Vanished

in

Bitterroot Mountains

James Kipling

Vanished in Bitterroot Mountains (Mystery and Suspense)

Table of Contents

Chapter 1

Northwestern Montana ran by both sides of the vehicle as agents Smith and Holliday travelled in silence. It was all very peaceful... suspiciously so.

"It's too quiet" Holliday said. "We should have back up." He twisted in his seat and scanned all around.

"That plane disappeared. I don't like it." His partner, Smith, disagreed.

"Let's just check out this ranch before we bring anyone else in. We've been searching for months and seen nothing." He kept on driving towards the ranch ahead.

The car turned onto the dirt road leading up to Kimble's ranch. They'd had a few leads that pointed to something going on here, but nothing was concrete.

The ranch looked bigger than it seemed from a distance, and the FBI agents could see large buildings running along the sides of the road. The place was listed as a cattle ranch, but they could see that it was much larger than normal for ranching. The main building rose up in the center of the ranch as they drove closer; barns and other work and support buildings were scattered around, creating the illusion of a small town. Smith slowed the car. As they looked closer, they noticed the buildings were run down, some even falling apart. The main house was in obvious need of repair. The whole place had a neglected look about it and showed no signs of being run as a working ranch. There was, however, someone sitting out on the front porch.

"Let's see what this guy has to say, but if this turns out to be another dead end, there's not much more we can do," Smith said. "We probably should have packed it in months ago."

The car pulled up in front of the main house and both agents climbed out. They were dressed casually, having learned the hard way that many locals didn't particularly love what the FBI represented.

The man on the porch was old and the wooden bench he sat on even older. He was smoking a pipe and looking at them from under his hat.

"Mr. Kimble?" Smith asked politely, but he stood in front of the car and his eyes took in the surrounding area carefully. It wouldn't be the first time someone in Montana chased them away with a shotgun.

"I'm Tom Smith and this is Matt Holliday. We wanted to ask you a few questions."

"Mr. Kimble?!" The old man laughed in a raspy voice. "No one has called me that in years. Everybody calls me Grandpa Joe."

"Nice to meet you, Grandpa Joe." Holliday smiled to put the old man at ease. "So, can we ask you a few questions?"

"About what?" The old man asked skeptically, and looked past them at the car. "Nobody comes around here much."

"Friend of ours is missing. He was in this area when he disappeared. We're just asking around if anyone had seen him," Smith glanced around. "I guess you would remember if someone different had been around."

"I don't talk to cops," Grandpa Joe said without a flicker while ignoring the question, "and you two look like cops to me."

"We're not the cops," Holliday said, trying to calm him. "We really are just looking for a friend."

"Don't believe you." The old man stood up from his bench slowly, taking his time extending his legs while holding his back. "You're trespassers! You should get off my land before I shoot you." By now the man was yelling and Holliday half turned to go. The old man looked anything but dangerous and they were obviously upsetting him. Smith put one foot on the first step of the porch in preparation to climb up.

"Look," he said, "we don't want trouble. Can you just tell us if you've seen any strangers around."

"Are you or are you not cops?" Grandpa Joe shouted.

"Answer me!" He pointed at them threateningly.

"Okay, okay." Holliday stepped forward and raised his hands in the universal sign of surrender. "No need to get worked up. We are not cops, and we'll be on our way,"

"Get off my property, now," Grandpa Joe yelled hysterically, "or I'll shoot you both. I'm going inside for my gun, and if you're still here when I come out, I'm going to shoot you."

Holliday looked at his friend and fellow agent, and they both sensed the old guy was hiding something. He was way too upset for the situation at hand. Something wasn't right here.

"Let's go, he's not going to talk to us," Smith said, in a voice plenty loud enough for the old man to hear.

"Okay," Holliday agreed, and they both made to turn around to walk back to the car. They had gone only a few steps when several camouflaged gunmen sprang from the side of the building and sprayed the agents with a hail of gunfire. They didn't even have a chance to reach for their guns before they were lying on the ground, full of bullet holes. The gunmen continued to shoot, enjoying the way their shots made the bodies' jump, as if they were still alive.

By the time Grandpa Joe returned to the porch with his antique rifle, two of the gunmen were dragging the bodies away and a third was climbing into their car. The old man just shook his head at the mess visible from his porch and sat back down on his bench. No one spoke as the place was meticulously cleaned of all evidence. Bullet shells were collected, bloody dirt vanished, the car was ditched and the bodies were disposed of. Grandpa Joe was left to enjoy his evening nap on his sunny porch with no more unwanted interruptions.

"They were getting too close," he said to himself, as he leaned back on the warm bench.

Chapter 2

Like most cities in the US, Salt Lake City was busy, noisy and not a nice place to attempt to run through. Special Agent Asa Clark was late for a meeting, but the city didn't care about her problems. The day had started off badly. She had woken up late, managed to spill coffee all over her clothes and then, on top of everything else, her car wouldn't start.

The city was busy early in the morning and she had to fight for a place on the bus line, run after two taxis, and take the stairs, because all the elevators were full. Sometimes her life really sucked.

She had managed to finish her last case successfully, though, sending a very astute killer to prison. He had terrorized a neighborhood for almost a year. The local media criticized the FBI for not being able to catch the killer, and Agent Clark had worked non-stop, to the point where own life had been put on hold.

Now that the case was behind her, she had thought that she'd have some time to relax and maybe even take a few days of vacation. But no, the Deputy Director had called her in after only two days and given her a new assignment.

Agent Clark rushed through the building, navigating her way to the office of Josie Shepherd, Deputy Director of the Criminal Enforcement Division. She was aware that the Deputy Director wasn't going to be happy about her being late. Stopping in front of the office door, Agent Clark took a few deep breaths and adjusted her suit jacket, hoping the meeting would be quick.

She knocked on the door and waited a few seconds, receiving no answer. "Deputy Director?" she called through the door.

"Come in. I've been waiting for some time now. You're late, Agent Clark." The voice was harsh and unfriendly.

Agent Asa Clark walked in and closed the door behind her, looking over at the woman sitting behind the heavy desk in front of the window. The Deputy Director was watching her coldly.

"I am really sorry I'm so late, Director Shepherd. I had problems with my car and had to take the—"

"Take a seat, Clark," the Director interrupted her.

"Yes sir," she answered quickly, addressing Director Shepherd the way she preferred. "Just sit," the Deputy Director instructed. She opened a file on her desk.

"I have a case for you." She didn't wait for a response and went on. "The one you just finished was a big one, but time for yourself will have to wait."

Agent Clark stayed silent, though she really didn't feel like taking a new case so soon.

"This case is very sensitive," the Deputy Director continued, not expecting an answer. "Two FBI field agents have disappeared in Montana. Agents Smith and Holliday were investigating a possible criminal organization in the area. Their last report was exactly one week ago today. Last Thursday, they contacted their Direct Supervisor. They informed him that they were going to visit some ranches in the region to check out the criminal activity in the area. They didn't contact him again three days later when they were due to give a status report. We have already had the local office check on them, but unfortunately, there is no sign of the two agents."

"So, you want me to investigate their disappearance?" Agent Clark asked, already switching gears and thinking of possible strategies to use in solving the case.

"Yes. Handle it with the utmost caution, professionalism and care," the Deputy Director instructed. Smith and Holliday are both good agents, with years of experience in the field. According to their boss, they were ready to close the case, as they just hadn't come up with any proof of the existence of a criminal or cartel related organization in the area."

"I'll be needing access to all the case files then," Clark answered, and was already in her work mode. "Did they have families?"

"Agent Smith is divorced and has no children, while Agent

Holliday has a fiancé and a mother at home," the other woman answered sadly, and for the first time that morning, showing some human emotion. "I want to find out what happened to them just as soon as we can."

"I understand," Agent Clark agreed. "I'll review the files today and head out to Montana this evening. I'll keep in touch and inform you of any new leads."

"Okay. Agent Clark, you're a good agent, and I have to congratulate you on your latest successfully closed case, but—" she paused. "I'm assigning you to a case that involves two of our own— always a hard thing to do. Be extra careful on this one, Agent. I have a gut feeling that something is going on out there. It feels all wrong and going in with fresh eyes, you just might spot it."

"Yes Sir. I'll look at all of the evidence and see what the locals have to say," Clark replied, "and hope we can find those two agents alive."

"Use the field office in Kalispell, Clark. They have some good people there. I understand you're already familiar with the area?"

"Yes. My mother is from the Salish Flathead Indian Reservation not far from there."

The Deputy Director pushed a stack of files across her desk. "Take these files. They have the notes from Smith and Holliday. You can always contact me, Agent. Even on my private phone if you find it necessary."

After a few more questions, Agent Clark took the files and walked out of the office. She had been working as a FBI agent for several years now and nothing really surprised her anymore. But when other agents were involved it brought an added urgency to the case.

Chapter 3

Asa Clark's plane touched down at Montana's regional airport in Kalispell late the next morning. It had taken her longer than she expected to go through the files. Thankfully, at least the flight had been a relaxing one, who took a moment to review the files and notes in her mind.

At the airport, she looked for a liaison, but nobody seemed to have come to meet her. She had contacted the local people to let them know she was on her way. Clark walked out of the airport and climbed into one of a handful of cabs that were sitting there.

The town of Kalispell was small but full of activity. She was familiar with the area but had grown up in a much larger city. The taxi driver was talking to her about a local fair where there was going to be racing and cattle pageants. She sighed and wondered what it was like to only have the local entertainment to worry about. Her job left very little time for anything lighthearted.

"Here we are," the driver announced happily, as he stopped the car in front of the bank building that held the Kalispell FBI field office. "It's up on the second floor. And don't forget about the fair."

Agent Clark entered the bank building and wasn't surprised when everyone greeted her with a good morning, or at least a smile. That was something you didn't see often in the big city.

Up the stairs to the second floor, she went through the door marked 'FBI' in large letters, and approached the front desk which was occupied by a middle-aged woman.

"I'm here for Agent Todd Gibson. He should be waiting for me," she said, taking off her glasses. "Agent Asa Clark."

"Agent Clark?" the woman asked. "We've been expecting you. I'll ask Todd if he can see you now."

Asa took a seat in the waiting area.

At twenty-nine, she was an attractive woman, although, not in the conventional way. She preferred to look professional, dressing in suits and conservative clothes. Her long dark hair was always tied back out of the way, because her work was the most important thing in her life and she wanted to be taken seriously. Asa had always dreamed of becoming an FBI agent. She joined the FBI Academy straight out of college and graduated with First Class Honors. Her sociology degree combined with her analytical intelligence helped her to solve cases that other agents found impossible.

With a Native American mother and an Irish father, Asa had done well to obtain her current success, overcoming the odds against her, perhaps. She was a perfectionist who loved detail. Her notes were meticulous and the many hours spent reviewing the cases she solved paid off with success. At the same time, though she was familiar to some extent with the area of the case, she had actually grown up in a big city. Clark liked the city lifestyle, but she could ride a bull if the occasion demanded, she loved to line dance when time allowed, sometimes drank a little too much and she was superbly fit. Her one concession to looking professionally chic and well-dressed on the job, was to wear shoes that would still allow her to break into a sprint when the situation demanded.

Right now, Asa Clark was a young FBI agent that people saw at the top of her game. She had solved a number of high profile cases by being thorough and paying attention to even the slightest detail. She had gained the attention of her superiors, who were eager to move her up the chain of command if she continued to prove herself. She wasn't surprised that a case involving two missing field agents was assigned to her, but she was no fool and could see that this might well be an extremely dangerous mission. A lot would depend on the people who worked here in the local area. As a bonus, her connection to the Native American culture nearby was a tool she could use during the investigation. In fact, her mother still had relatives right here in Kalispell.

"Agent Clark?!" The woman behind the desk called out. "Agent Gibson will see you now." Asa stood up and the other woman continued, "His office is on the left, you'll see his name on the door."

"Thank you," Clark said, and followed her directions. Gibson's office was easy to find and she softly knocked on the open door as she entered.

"Agent Gibson, my name is Agent Asa Clark," she said formally. "I've been assigned to help with the case of the two missing agents."

"Ah, Clark, you finally arrived," the man sitting behind the desk said. "Come in, come in, there's a lot to discuss."

"Agent Gibson," Clark wanted to show that she had authority in the situation. "I was assigned the case and was told that you would be a great help to me."

"Correct. We need to solve this case urgently, and working together we are going to get that done." He gave her a brief smile that transformed the worried look on his face and made him look approachable and friendly. "Smith and Holliday were onto something and we need to find out what that was which will lead us to them." She nodded and agreed.

"I'll be needing the reports you have from the case they were working on," Asa told him. "I've gone through everything my boss had, but you'll have more detail here." Gibson nodded.

"We have the reports waiting for you and a desk to use as your own. Once you've had a chance to look at them, we can talk about how to make a start."

"Thanks," Clark answered, and Gibson stood up and opened the door to show her to her new workspace.

A desk had been assigned to her for her time in Montana, and the secretary brought in the reports. She then showed her around the small office and pointed out the coffee machine.

The sooner she could get down to solving this case, the better, Asa thought. It was clear that the two missing agents were in trouble, and she hoped they would be found alive. Privately, she thought it unlikely, and the look on Gibson's face told her that he probably felt the same way. There was no time to lose as she gratefully got some coffee and set out to scan through the reports.

Chapter 4

Asa spent the rest of the day reviewing the paperwork generated by the two missing agents. As she worked, details began to immerge. Slowly, she began to understand their case. Smith and Holliday had been investigating the possible existence of a criminal drug organization working in western Montana with ties to the Mexican drug cartels.

They had conducted many interviews around the region, just old fashioned footwork, but they had used technology and scoured the internet for clues as well. They had recorded it all and she soon enough she started to see a pattern.

"Shit," Agent Clark said, quietly to herself.

She went through the files until the words were ingrained in her mind. It wasn't obvious at first. The accidents seemed random, a series of unfortunate events in rural Montana, which had more cattle than people. Each of the events were noted by the agents and categorized by date and geographical position.

Smith and Holliday had red flagged a few small towns and ranches in the area after finding some minor connections. Clark surmised that it had probably been more gut feeling on the part of the agents than actual evidence. They had made several trips around western Montana, doing research and asking questions. However, after months of work they still had nothing solid.

The lack of hard evidence and no obvious pattern to the incidents, effectively threw the local police off the scent. There was just enough suspicion that the FBI took over the investigation. They acted carefully, never letting people know that they were interested in the case. Whoever was behind the terrorist acts wouldn't expect anyone to be looking into the case after the police had given up. Asa Clark intended to keep it that way.

The secretary, Ann Shrump, had tried to help Asa with the files and was happy to let her know what she had picked up from the missing agents.

"Here we have a list of small fires started near local buildings," Shrump told her. "All the fires have passed as accidents, except for the fact that there is a distinct pattern." She went on.

"Tom, erm, I mean Agent Smith, thought that each criminal involved had their own job, like their own area of expertise. He suspected the same person had started all the fires, and likewise, another who dealt with the cars. He even thought it was a different person who was doing the shooting at those in the area."

"Yeah, that sounds logical," Asa agreed. "But, how do we find these people? They seem to be all over the county."

"Someone around here has to have an idea of what is going on," Ann added, pointing at the notes on the table.

"I bet Agent Smith thought so too," Asa agreed.

Ann left shortly after that, leaving Asa alone to deal with the reports. She stretched her arms slowly upwards and sighed in relief as her body seemed to relax. Her legs were hurting from sitting in the same position for so long, but Asa was ready to stay the whole night if needed. She had already found a hotel nearby and made a reservation. Her luggage was waiting for her by the front desk and Ann had assured her that the hotel was only a short walk from the office. Kalispell was a small and compact town.

Around four in the afternoon, Asa decided to take a break and went to her hotel to check in, grab a shower and get something to eat. The day had been filled with too many surprises and unanswered questions for her taste. Even away from the FBI office, she couldn't stop thinking about the case, looking for somewhere to start her investigation and unravel the clues.

With her luggage in her room and now changed into something more comfortable, Asa couldn't face wearing her usual suit after she had spent the whole day on the plane and in the office. The office building was only a few blocks away, so she decided to walk back. It felt good to stretch her legs and get some fresh air.

She was greeted by the same lady behind the front desk, who

was surprised to see her back so soon and recommended she get some rest. Asa smiled at her genuine concern, but assured her that she was okay and that there was work to get started on.

Nearly everyone in the office had left by that point, except Gibson and herself. Within ten minutes of reading through the files again, Asa realized that there was nothing more to be learned from them. Someone cleared their throat behind her and Asa jerked her head up. Gibson was walking in her direction, pulling on his jacket and looking ready to go home.

"Isn't it time to wrap it up for the day?" Gibson asked her.

"Yes, you're probably right," Asa agreed. "Did you know that most of the information in these files was collected without sourcing? There are no names attached to each quote. It's confusing and hard to follow up."

"That's how small towns work," Gibson replied. "People are always in each other's pockets. You run the risk of everyone ganging up on you if you say the wrong thing to the wrong person. Smith and Holliday knew that."

"Ah yes. It means that we will have to start the investigation all over again," Asa said, but she thought it was still sloppy work and it niggled at her.

After retracing all the data, Clark was convinced that the case wasn't going to be as simple as it had seemed to her at the beginning.

"Come on, let's go get something to eat. We can talk things over and get a good start in the morning," Gibson offered, as a way to introduce her to the town. "I know the perfect place."

Chapter 5

The country bar and grill was nearly filled with customers, all locals from the looks of it. Gibson seemed to be known to everyone and the two of them had to stop at more than one table to answer questions and greet people. Asa saw one of the perks of the small town, and smiled at the way people welcomed her. They simply allowed folks to assume they were just friends. It seemed the logical thing to do, and it was surprising what people talked about when they were relaxed.

The bar seemed like a fun place for the local people, and the two FBI agents chose a table at the back, away from the big crowd. The bar was divided into two sections – one child-friendly, and another for adults, where they could drink and have some fun. Everything was innocent enough and Asa examined the menu with interest, choosing a steak and baked potato. The two of them ate in comfortable silence, until their hunger was subdued.

"You're probably wondering about the town and the people, huh?" Gibson started. "This is rural country with ranchers and farmers who keep our feet on the ground. Most of the people here work on the ranches in the outer area and keep to themselves. Ironically." He laughed, and explained, "This is the kind of town where everybody knows everybody, but they all mind their own business."

"I noticed," Asa commented. "You seem to have a lot of friends in here."

"Yeah, I wouldn't call them friends, mostly acquaintances. But, you're right, it is difficult to stay hidden."

"I can't say that I know the people here, but I am somewhat familiar with the area," Asa commented. "My mother, she's from the Salish Flathead Reservation," she added.

"Really, then you're practically family. In that case, you should definitely call me Todd." Laughing, he went on, "I used to spend a lot of time in the Salish reserve, and I have a lot of friends there."

"My mother was Salish, and taught me a lot about the Native American way of life. I suppose the Deputy Director sent me here because of my connection to the area."

"I'm sure that it will help you, especially once you start interrogating people and driving around the country." Todd smiled. "Look at him, for example," he said, and nodded towards a man who sat two tables away from them eating a plate full of ribs. "He is typical Montana, and you are very safe around people like him."

"You can't tell by looking at people, though. A normal front can hide a lot of trouble," she retorted. "I've learned long ago not to take folks at face value," she looked around the room, thinking.

"Tell me, Todd," Asa suddenly changed the subject. "Do you think Smith and Holliday are already dead?"

Her serious tone brought the situation into sharp focus, and he looked up at her, taking his time and drinking from his glass before answering.

"Yes… I do. I wish I didn't, but I do," he said in the same serious tone of voice. "I already searched the area for them twice, and although there is still a chance we'll find them alive, I doubt it. There have been similar cases in the area, not with agents, but with a cop, a bank manager and even a local ranch hand. The three of them disappeared and were never found."

"All three of them together?" Asa asked him, very interested in the information.

"No. But now I'm not so sure that their cases are unrelated after all," Todd said, looking grim.

Asa nodded her head in agreement. For a long minute, she thought about his words, and she also thought about how she was feeling after reading the files. She looked back at the man he had pointed out and watched him eating in silence, completely ignoring the other people in the bar.

Asa wondered if she was going to become like him after a

few years... alone. She just might if she continued to say no to all the men who expressed interest in her, then she wondered why that particular thought had suddenly entered her mind.

"Okay, enough with the gloomy thoughts. What do you do for fun in the big city, Agent Clark?" Todd suddenly asked.

Asa laughed at his comment. "Call me Asa, please. Well, what can I say? I like live music, dancing, going on hikes, the usual stuff."

"Okay then, what do you say we move over to the bar." Todd stood up after leaving a few banknotes on the table and finishing his beer. "There's a pretty good local band starting up on the stage pretty soon."

Asa laughed and agreed. The man wasn't as bad as she had originally thought. Todd Gibson was acting like an old friend right now, which helped her relax and enjoy herself a bit. They walked together to the bar and sat at the only two seats available. Sitting back and enjoying the music as it played, she discovered they had similar taste in music and a few other things. Asa decided to take the evening for what it was, relax a bit, and start work seriously the next morning. Although, she was getting a feel for the local people anyway, and having a pleasant time to boot.

They were about to call it a day when an argument broke out across the bar. A big man was objecting to being told to settle down and go home, and he was starting to break up the glassware. Some customers ran for cover and others tried to help the bar workers escort the man outside. It turned very rapidly into a bar brawl and Todd Gibson reluctantly stood up to go help. Asa realized she would have to back him up, and between them they managed to subdue the very large and drunken customer. But on the way to the door, he suddenly wrenched himself free, grabbed a bottle and smashed it over Todd's head who sank to the floor.

Asa slammed the man's arm up his back and booted him out the door where he crashed onto the sidewalk.

"Get the local police to pick him up," she told the barman,

and rushed back to help Gibson to his feet. He was a bit groggy but in one piece, and after sitting on a chair for a few minutes he insisted he was fine to go home and wouldn't need an ambulance.

Asa tried not to offer to help him walk and just made sure he was steady on his feet. He made for his car and she took over.

"I'll drive you home," she declared, and insisted in such a way that he didn't object. He gave in gracefully and handed over the keys. He complained about feeling like such a fool, but she drove where he directed and told him that anyone would go down with a crash on the head like that one.

His house was not large but turned out to be clean and tidy. She took in the general feel of the place, noted there were no womanly touches, refused a late-night coffee and suggested he take something for the headache he was bound to have.

"Your head will hurt after that blow, but at least it's not bleeding," She knew it was a very short walk to the hotel, so she told him they would start work on the case in the morning and left him on the sofa with a glass of water and the tablets in his hand. She was beginning to like Todd Gibson and thought that maybe they would be able to work as a team to solve the case after all.

Chapter 6

The next morning, Todd woke up on the sofa feeling sore. His first movements felt like knives going through his head, but after he managed to drag himself to the bathroom, take a piss, and drink some water, he started feeling like a human being again.

"Shit, shit, shit..." he continued to repeat throughout the whole procedure, and was thinking of Asa and the case. He felt that he had not looked so good the night before.

A hot shower cleared his mind and he realized he needed to be at work in less than an hour. He hurried to get dressed and finally stepped outside the house. His car was parked in front of the house instead of in the garage, where he usually kept it. His walk to the office was a short one.

Before heading to the office, Todd stopped at his favorite cafe and bought a coffee and a dozen pastries for the office, something he would not even dream about any other day of the week, but today was special. *You can learn a lot from a local cafe,* Todd thought to himself, as he left carrying the pastries and coffee. He had even gone to the trouble of passing the time of day with the girl behind the counter as he waited for his order.

Agent Todd Gibson was fifty-four years old, five foot and eight inches tall and a bit larger in the waist than he would have liked. He liked his profession and tried hard to look the part, dressing in good quality suits and caring for his appearance. After graduating from the FBI Academy, he had been transferred from one office to the other for a number of years. Five years ago, he was assigned to the Kalispell Office and with that, had finally found his place in the world.

Gibson really liked the quiet, rural way of life in Montana and didn't miss the faster pace of the big cities at all. But lately, he was feeling tired and that made him look forward to retirement.

For him it had been always important to have a good job, to be respected and preferably to be in a position of some authority. With the arrival of Asa Clark in his office, Todd's job was to ensure she had the tools she needed to work the case.

As Todd Gibson entered the office, he took a file from his secretary, raised his hand at another agent and went into his office.

Agent Asa Clark was knocking on his office door before he had time to sit down behind his desk.

"How's the head?" she asked, and when he looked fine she went right on, saying, "The police just informed us that they found a vehicle nearby, in the Kootenai National Forest. It's Smith and Holliday's car, and they have it at the impound lot."

"Shit," Gibson cursed soundly. "That is bad news."

"Yeah, it's looking pretty bad for them," Clark agreed. "I'm headed out to go examine the car, are you coming?"

"Yes, let's go," Todd said, quickly getting up from his chair and reaching for his jacket.

He grabbed a car from the FBI pool and drove Clark to the impound lot. The police had found the dumped car the previous day, but it hadn't been identified until that morning. There was no sign of the two FBI agents, but Asa hoped to find some leads in the car.

The car showed no signs of an accident or of something violent happening inside. That was both good and bad news for them, but the agents didn't make any assumptions and just started to work. Asa put on a pair of gloves and started her examination of the car. She worked methodically, taking prints of the tire treads, lifting fingerprints from various locations inside the car, and taking fabric samples and hairs from the seats.

She had experience with forensics and knew which key details to examine. There was no saying what a car could tell you if you knew where to look for it. Unfortunately, there was no paper trail, identification or any other documents that could connect the car to the agents. It was theirs, no doubt about that, but it seemed that they didn't leave anything behind,

Once the material collected was sent to the lab, Clark and Gibson took a break, standing in front of the lot and drinking cups of strong black coffee.

"Things don't look good," Agent Clark stated. "The car was dumped, but not burned or hidden. Someone has taken their documents, but left behind the car documentation and numbers, so it was really simple to identify it. They either didn't care or simply... I don't know what. Maybe whoever did it is so confident of their situation that they felt no need to destroy it completely. "

"Yeah..." Gibson took a sip from his coffee. "It seems more confusing than before. If someone killed them, why dump the car, but not the bodies? If they're alive, why didn't they come forward? If someone is holding them, why haven't we found any leads as to where? There's been no ransom request... "

"Yes," Clark agreed, throwing her empty coffee cup in the bin. "Maybe we should change the way we work the case. Maybe we should approach it from a different angle."

"Yeah, maybe." Gibson said, and headed towards the car.

Chapter 7

Asa and Todd returned to the field office together and once again looked through the case files. There must be some hidden kernel of truth in them somewhere, but it was escaping their attention. She had memorized nearly every word in those files, but she still wasn't able to fit the pieces together.

Gibson finally went back to his office, leaving Clark to deal with the case on her own.

She took an hour break for lunch and then returned to the office to plan her next move. She asked Ann for assistance and decided to move the investigation to the next logical place, the city morgue. She had already been assigned a car, so she drove the ten blocks to the morgue.

The place was just the same as the many other morgues she had visited over the years, but it still made her shiver. She hated the sight of death and the smell of it. In her mind, the smell of antiseptic was connected to the image of dead bodies. Asa took a deep breath and walked inside the building, heading directly to the front desk.

"Hello," she greeted the woman behind the desk and took out her FBI badge. "Agent Clark, FBI. Can you tell me if any John Does have been brought in?"

The woman looked carefully at her badge, then lowered her gaze to the computer in front of her. "I will call the manager for you, Agent Clark," she said politely. "I don't have the authority to release that information on my own without a supervisor."

Asa agreed to wait and walked in the direction the woman pointed. The smell of disinfectant here was even stronger, but the agent started to get used to it and resolved to ignore it. The manager didn't make her wait for long, and the FBI agent was called into his office by the time she made it down the hall to his door.

"Agent Clark." The middle-aged man offered his hand. "I'm Dr. Richards. How can I help you?"

"Nice to meet you, Doctor." Asa returned the handshake and sat down in the chair he offered. "I need information about any unidentified bodies that have arrived at the morgue in the last week."

"Sorry Agent, but we haven't seen a body in weeks," the man commented. "In fact, the last few months has been very peaceful, with only expected deaths of the elderly and such."

"I see," Asa said, both relieved and disappointed. The morgue was just another dead end. "Well, thank you anyway, and please, contact me directly if there is anything new to report." Doctor Richards promised to do just that and accompanied Asa out of the morgue.

The FBI agent took her time walking to the car. The case was getting more and more complex without anything of note happening. The very few leads she had were leading her nowhere, so she went back over in her mind what she usually did when solving a case.

"What should I do now?" Asa asked herself, frustrated at the lack of evidence. Deciding that going back to review the files again would be a waste of time, so she headed towards the center of the city. Unsure of what to do next and wanting to clear her head, Asa decided to take a walk and look around the main street of the town. She rolled her eyes at the very idea of Asa Clark shopping for fun.

People were walking all around her and bemused, Asa wondered to herself as the people noticed her, smiled and often shared a nod, wave or cheery greeting.

"Enough," she said to herself. "Back to the computer and searching the internet for connections to the fires, the disappearances and the missing agents." She retrieved the car and went back to the office, wondering if there would be any staff available to help her search the web.

Chapter 8

The next morning, Asa woke up after a good night's sleep, ready to start work anew. The incident in the bar from first night was forgotten, the dead ends of yesterday from the car and the morgue chalked up as part of the larger story. Her determination to solve the case had returned with a new force. She showered, dressed, ate her breakfast quickly and was already planning her tactics as she left the hotel. The walk to the FBI field office was relaxing and Asa used the atmosphere to gather her strength for the hours to follow. She had already decided what to do next, and that was giving her the confidence to face Gibson again.

"Agent Gibson, oh sorry—Todd," she greeted him as she entered his office. "I'm all loaded up and ready to go out to the site where the car was found."

She had already called ahead and informed him of her plans for the day and Gibson had agreed to take her out to where a local farmer had found the car.

"I'll be with you in ten minutes, make sure we have everything we might need. We'll want to take some food and drinks—we won't find any cafes out there."

Agent Clark walked back out, closing the door behind her and double checking the provisions.

Gibson was ready half an hour later and climbed into the car without another word. Asa put the car into motion and drove away, heading towards the national forest. She had already checked out the direction, so there was no need to ask questions or pick up a conversation. According to the map, it was going to take a good two hours to reach the site where the car was dumped. It looked as if it was going to be a long and potentially quiet drive.

After they left the city and drove out through the valley a ways, Asa couldn't help but notice the towering mountain ranges on either side of them. She remarked on how wonderful the scenery was just to break the silence and Gibson agreed that it was magnificent.

"So, tell me about yourself." Todd broke the silence as they drove on.

"What do you want to know?" she asked, surprised.

"We have a two-hour drive in front of us," Gibson commented. "I'm just looking for something to talk about."

"How's your head today?" she asked in return, and he gave her a rueful grin.

"Come on… anything but that!" Chuckling, he said, "Turns out that was quite a crack he gave me, but apart from the headache, it seems okay."

She drove in silence for a bit, obviously in thought, so he didn't interrupt.

"Okay, let's see, what can I tell you about myself?" She decided to try to open up. "I am a big city girl, but as I told you the other day, my mother is from this area. She made sure to teach me about the earth and how important it is to stay connected to it. I am very proud of my origins, if that is what you want to know. When I was young, I used to spend every summer with my mother's family by Flathead Lake. It was something I always looked forward to and taught me how to stay grounded."

"Geez, I'm almost jealous," Todd admitted. "The most exciting thing I did during my childhood was go to a space camp."

"I am sorry to hear that," Asa said, laughing. "But actually, I kind of always wanted to go to a space camp." Gibson laughed at her comment and she continued.

"When I finished college, I went to Quantico and became an FBI agent. The rest, as they say, is history. So tell me, how long have you served at the field office here in Kalispell?"

Gibson easily started his own story.

"It's already been five years since I was sent to this office," he shared. "But I really like it here. It's different here, you know? The atmosphere or something. There was a time when I longed for more excitement, but now I'm more than happy with the job. Small towns and knowing all the locals suits me fine these days."

"Lucky you," Asa commented. "It's not that often that I meet people who love what they are doing."

"I never said I love it, just that I'm happy with it. Content, I guess." Gibson laughed at her assumption. "I'm just normal really. With the passing of the years, I have learned to be happy... no, content... with what I have."

"And the people here? What do you think about them?" Asa continued to ask questions.

"Oh, the people." He moved his head up and down, as if contemplating his answer. "They are something, aren't they? When I first came here it was hard to see through the first impression, but with time I got used to it. To the chatting, to the complete lack of privacy, to the constant presence of someone who thinks they know me. Yet they clam up if I ask a question. They did come to accept me in the end, though. I think."

"I can see that." Asa thought about what he was saying. "I noticed what you described, although everyone is so nice. It's like they go out of their way or something... yet—"

"Uh-oh, look!" Gibson pointed at a dirt road coming up on their right. "We're almost there. Turn right up here."

Asa looked around at the tall trees and green bushes that surrounded them. Birds sang happily up in the branches and there was a soft wind blowing warm and fresh, lifting the leaves and making them dance. The place looked almost familiar to her, and Asa thought of the many days she had spent living with her mother's family during the summer.

She parked the car beside a group of trees and they stepped out, careful not to miss anything. The area had already been searched already, and both of them had studied the photographic evidence, but there was always the possibility that something had been missed.

Everything looked straightforward, though. The car had been left on the side of the dirt road. The key was in the ignition, and one of the doors was open. Because of the dry conditions, there weren't any particularly interesting prints in the dirt, but according to the forensic team, there had been another car which had turned around and went back the same way it had come.

Gibson had already called the local authorities and they were sending the park rangers, who were among the first on the scene. The two men soon arrived, while Clark and Gibson were still looking around.

"Hi, guys," Gibson greeted them. "This is Agent Clark and I am Agent Gibson. We wanted to talk to you once more about finding the car."

"Rangers Stevens and Fynn," one of them said, as the four of them shook hands. "What do you want to know?"

"Just to confirm we understand the sequence and all, you were the first ones on the scene, after the farmer called nine-one-one?" Asa asked them.

"Yes," Ranger Fynn answered. "We arrived less than an hour after the call came in. The man was still here, but he really had nothing to tell us. We ran the car numbers and found out that it was listed in the police bulletin, so we secured the area and called for the forensic team."

"Did you notice anything or anyone out of the ordinary?" Clark asked again.

The two rangers looked at each other and used a few moments to think about the question. This time it was Ranger Stevens who decided to answer, "We noticed nothing strange, apart from the car itself. You can see the area, it's so out of the way here that it's safe to say that only two or three cars pass by here in a week, if that. When we arrived, all we could see was the car. Nothing else, no people, no prints, no other objects. I still think that whoever dumped the vehicle here came in with another car and did the job quickly."

"Yeah, that seems the most likely explanation, but still, it's never too much to ask new questions," Gibson said, joining the conversation for the first time.

The ranger asked them if there was anything else they could do for them and left soon after. Clark and Gibson stayed at the site and continued to analyze it. Asa made sure to do the job properly and was rewarded with the finding of a few fresh hoof prints, clearly left by a horse.

"Is this strange?" she called to Gibson. "No one mentioned these prints before."

"In Montana horses are more common than cars," Gibson commented. "The forensic team probably thought they were unrelated to the case."

Asa didn't make the same mistake and made sure to photograph and measure the prints carefully. She also got a clear picture of the manufacturers mark from one of the horseshoes. After that, little else needed to be said. As if there was an unspoken agreement that the job was complete, both agents climbed into the car and they drove away.

Chapter 9

Once they arrived back at the FBI office, Asa was restless and felt as if she was on fire. The work day was almost over by the time they got back, but she wasn't ready to give up yet. So, instead of writing her report for the day and going home, she followed Agent Gibson into his office with a copy of the hoof print she'd printed out.

"You should send this off to be identified right away," she told him. Gibson had other things on his desk that needed his immediate attention, but he had been impressed by the way Asa talked the job. He bit back his instinctive retort about doing it the next day and took the folder that she was holding out.

"Our lab is pretty good," he told her. "If I flag it as urgent they'll do their best," Asa thanked him.

"When agents are missing, everybody pulls out the stops," she said. He asked if she would like to go to the lab and meet the team there personally. She thought that would be a good idea, plus she'd be able to see if they were likely to get the job done quickly.

"I'll go back to the lot and have another go at the car after the visit to the lab," she told him. "I can follow you in my car, and that way you can get back here to finish any other work you need to wrap up tonight." He gave her a slow smile as he realized that she had in fact understood that he was putting off other priorities in order to get her request processed as soon as possible.

"Right then, let's go," he said, grabbing his jacket from the chair where he had dropped it on the way in. "You follow, and I'll be coming back here as soon as I introduce you. Give me a ring if you come up with anything."

The laboratory turned out to be an up to the minute affair with four people working in white coats and surrounded by what appeared to be excellent equipment. Asa was introduced to the staff, and as planned, Gibson left to return to his office. She held out the folder with the print of the horseshoe.

"This might be nothing, but we don't have much to go on and I would appreciate your thoughts. We inspected the site where the car from the missing agents was left and I found some hoof prints. There is a mark on one shoe." A man named Martin took the offered file and scrutinized the mark with a magnifying glass.

"It's pretty clear, so we should be able to narrow it down somewhat," he said with a smile. She found herself thinking that maybe this team would be a good one after all.

"Give me your mobile number and as soon as we come up with anything, I'll give you a buzz." She smiled back and gave him the number.

"I'm going back to have another look at the car. I'll leave you to it. Thanks."

Asa went back to the lot where the car was still being held. She proceeded to remove the brake and gas pedals, intending to analyze them in greater detail. She wanted to check for a possible boot or shoe print. One of the local police officers helped her with the removal of the pedals.

"Thank you. I appreciate the help very much," she told him. "Did you know the missing agents?" The officer said that he knew Tom Smith, and that the man was a decent sort of guy.

"He was not particularly happy about going on with the investigation and he always liked backup."

"So, they didn't let anyone know where they were going?" she asked, and he told her that he hadn't heard that anyone knew where they were headed. Asa tucked away that information and took the pedals they had removed.

"I'm hoping the lab might find a clue as to what sort of soil is on them, or there might even be a boot print," she said. "It might narrow the search down somehow."

"Everything's worth a try," the man told her and waved as she drove away. The lab techs were still at work and said they would try soil tests straight away.

"Whoever drove the car to where it was dumped might have

come from a particular area," she said, and the forensic people agreed.

"We have to try everything," Martin told her, and she left to go back to the office to update Gibson on what she done. He was still at his desk, but pushed the papers to one side when she entered the room.

"The lab was really helpful," she told him. "I left them the two pedals from the car to test for soil identification or boot prints, and they said they would get straight on it." Gibson agreed that they were always helpful.

"Come on, I'll buy you a coffee or something, and we can think about what the next step should be." Despite the work still on his desk, he made the suggestion, and she was happy to accept. It would be good to talk it over and she wondered what his opinion of Tom Smith would be. Settled in at the diner with a latte and a sinfully sweet muffin, she told him what the officer had said and asked him why the agents hadn't kept anyone in the picture about where they were going.

"Come on, you've been at this for a while. You know what field agents are like." he sighed. "I did try and talk to them, but Hollister always liked to play things very close. It was like pulling teeth trying to get anything useful out of him before an investigation was complete."

"Can you remember anything that might give us a clue as to the general direction they were headed? They had written up the fire sites that they had visited, so maybe we can eliminate all of those and see what areas they hadn't been to before." Gibson thought that Asa Clark was at her best when she was completely obsessed by the investigation. This woman would not give up the search easily, and it had been many years since he had seen this sort of determination in action accompanied by the passion he could see in her eyes. He was impressed by her and actually found himself seeing her as a woman as well as an agent.

"Good thinkin' Batman," he told her. "Tomorrow, we'll get

the whole lot out on a map and see where they hadn't been before, and who knows, maybe the soil will match up with those areas or something."

"Thanks," Asa said, and stood up to go. "I think I need to crash and start out fresh in the morning. I'll buy the coffees the next time." They separated outside the diner and went to their separate cars. Asa realized at some point that she was really very tired.

Chapter 10

The next morning, Asa opened her eyes to a white ceiling. The now familiar noises of the town around her coupled with the warmth of the bed made her feel secure, and she was in that lovely comfortable sleepy place that makes you want to stay in bed all day. She shifted a bit and allowed herself another ten minutes, watching as the sun painted the room in beautiful shadows. Her body ached from the long hours yesterday, but she eventually made the move to start the day. It took her almost half an hour to get ready for the day and get settled for a cup of coffee in the local cafe. This place was a long way from home, but Asa was used to living this way and wasn't complaining.

The ringing of her phone gave her a start and almost made her spill her coffee. She quickly took the offending object out of her pocket and looked to see who was calling. The caller ID revealed that it was Deputy Director Shepherd on the phone.

"Shit!" she exclaimed, and put down her cup, preparing for a hard conversation with her boss.

"Agent Clark," she answered, grateful that her voice sounded normal again.

"Agent Clark," the woman on the other end of the line repeated. "You were supposed to call me yesterday. How is it that I had to learn that the car of the missing agents had been found from someone other than you?"

"Yes Sir," Asa agreed. "I'm sorry. I was trying to set the operation in motion, and was hoping to have more to report. What I have is damn little at this point. The car of the two agents was found, but so far it has given us no clues about what happened. I visited the site where the car was dumped, but was only able to retrieve the print of a horse hoof, which could be completely unrelated to the case. I left the pedals for soil analysis and the lab people seem to be efficient."

Agent Clark was speaking fast and straight to the point, not leaving the Deputy Director the time to add something or ask questions. She described the situation in the Montana field office, adding how helpful they had been.

"Thank you for the briefing, Agent Clark. See to it that next time, you are the one making the call," the director instructed. "I am not sure what you think ranch life and small towns are like, but ranches and farms these days depend on the digital world, there is a community college and an extension of Montana State U. in Kalispell, and they do have such modern conveniences as phones that could be tapped." The Director was firing on all cylinders. "Any sign of the agents or their bodies?"

"Nothing, we have found no evidence that they have been killed," Asa answered. "However, any hopes of finding them alive that I may have harbored are quickly starting to disappear."

"My suggestion is to try and blend in more with the locals, so that you can use them as a resource," Asa's boss suggested. "Now that you have seen the reports, examined the car and processed the site, you should start working the trail."

Asa agreed and listened to her instructions for another ten minutes. The Deputy Director was very interested in the outcome of the case and insisted that Clark call her every day with an update. Once the call was over, Asa ate some toast and headed out. Despite the lack of clues, there was much to be done. First, she went by the FBI office and checked to see if the results from the hoof prints and the pedals were ready. Ann assured her that she would call if they came in and Asa walked back out, ready for the next step of her plan.

Deputy Director Josie Shepherd, in her overly professional and commanding tone, had given her the boost in confidence she needed to approach the local people and talk to them for information. Shepherd had used her position and authority to make sure that Agent Clark would pull out all the stops. She usually found that it worked to be dominant and give directives. She knew that Clark was good and she would check over all of the present information and set out to talk to the locals. She fully expected to have more information before the end of the day.

Chapter 11

Later in the evening, Asa headed down to one of the pool halls in the town. She had left her FBI badge behind and dressed in a comfortable pair of jeans, a silk top and a jacket that made her look sophisticated, but not easy.

For the first time since she had arrived in town, Asa left her hair down and put on some make up.

The receptionist had given her directions to the pool hall, assuring her that this was the best place to meet the locals. Asa decided to do just that. She was going to make some friends there tonight!

The pool hall was exactly what she expected and Asa quickly found her way to the bar and ordered a beer. The place was filled with people who were shooting pool, drinking, and talking. She approached two of the groups and both welcomed her.

Asa didn't lose her courage and did the next logical thing, she started playing pool. She easily found a small group that accepted her request to join them and in no time, was beating them. Asa had learned how to play pool from an old friend in college and still remembered a few tricks. The locals continued to warm up to her and soon Asa had made a few friends.

"Come on, Asa," Lilly Huston was shouting at her. "You have to tell us, how do you do it? I have never seen a woman beat my Rich at pool."

Asa laughed at her enthusiasm and leaned over the pool table to give her final shot. Rich was completely defeated.

"Oh, sorry Lilly, but my secrets are my own. If I tell you, I will lose half of my advantage."

The rest of the people around the table laughed and Asa relaxed a little, feeling like maybe she could fit in. "I am going to get another beer," she told them after a while and headed over to the bar.

That was when she met him.

The man was standing alone at the bar, drinking beer and looking lost in his thoughts. He was maybe six feet tall, with dark blond hair and deep gray eyes. Asa's professional eye placed his age somewhere between thirty and thirty-five, while his clothes immediately spoke of a rancher or a farmer.

She leaned against the bar, just beside him, and the young man turned to look at her with a friendly smile on his lips. The moment their eyes met, there was an instant attraction between them and Asa could tell it was mutual.

"Gabriel Kimble," the man offered a hand to her, never breaking eye contact.

"Asa Clark," she answered, accepting his hand.

"I saw you beating Rich Hall on the table," he continued, letting her hand go slowly.

"Yeah, that was a sight all right," Asa agreed seriously, and ordered a beer from the bartender. "Can I buy you another one?"

"Isn't it my job to offer you a drink?"

"Uh-oh… everybody around here think women should cook the bacon instead of bring it home, or just you?" she threw right back at him.

"No ma'am, you got me all wrong. I'm just not used to seeing a woman who wants to pay, that is something else," The man laughed, then took the offered beer, making a show of drinking from it. "Thank you. Man, I really needed that."

"Are you from around here?" Asa asked easily, already feeling comfortable around the man.

"Yes and no," Gabriel answered. "I live on a ranch a few miles from the city, but for tonight I am staying at a hotel."

"That sounds interesting," the woman commented. "Is it a cattle ranch? I always wanted to see one."

"Consider yourself always invited to the Kimble Ranch," the man said gallantly. "Just be open-minded and don't expect too much."

"Have you always lived there? I'm not sure I would be able to live my whole life in one place."

"Me too," Gabriel Kimble agreed. "I've always dreamed of seeing the world, finding love, and having a greater destiny than a cattle ranch."

"Oh, such big dreams. It's going to take some time to fulfill them all. You better start right away!"

"If only it was so easy." The man shook his head. "But, maybe if I found the right woman, I would be able to man up and go against the very strong will of my older brother."

"One of those. I know the feeling."

After that, things went quickly. Gabriel invited her to his motel room and Asa was unable to say no. The room was typical… clean and tidy. Asa could say that the man hadn't spent too much time in here. With a dull, heavy thud, Gabriel shoved her against the door, leaning against her and claiming her lips in a passionate kiss.

At first, Asa thought she should protest, but the words caught in her throat when their lips locked together and the man pushed her jacket off her shoulders. The door clicked shut behind them, and their ragged panting was loud in the silence of the room. Outside cars were honking and tires were screeching and street sounds continued, but both were oblivious to anything but each other.

Asa's eyes were shut and she blocked everything else out, including the sounds of motel guests in the hall. Instead she held Gabriel's head, her hands curled tightly in his hair as he kissed her. His hands had vanished under her top, caressing her naked skin. Asa made an impatient sound, enjoying his hands on her body and wanting more. Gabriel ran his hands over her, caressing her belly, squeezing her bottom and slowly raising her top up to her armpits. He was trying to undress her without putting any distance between their bodies, and that made Asa smile against his lips.

"Let me help you," she murmured softly, when his lips descended to her neck. She pushed him gently away and slowly raised her arms up, so he could remove her top. Gabriel smiled at her and used the position to remove his own jacket and shirt, showing his muscular chest and shoulders. "You are beautiful," she whispered and the man laughed, stepping back and tugging her with him.

"Never tell a man he is beautiful," he said playfully, while removing her jeans and doing the same with his own. "We are either ruggedly handsome or hot, but never beautiful."

"You continue to tell yourself that, if it makes you feel better," Asa answered him as she let him lay her down on the bed.

Chapter 12

The next day, Asa woke up late in the morning, feeling happy and content. The night with Gabriel had gone better than she had expected and she hadn't returned to her own hotel until the early hours of the day.

They were both breathing hard and Asa felt as if she was going to explode from the adrenaline racing through her blood. Their kiss started slowly, with the man nipping at her lips and tracing them with his own. Gabriel used his tongue, silently asking to be let in. Asa opened her lips and Gabriel dove in, devouring her mouth and examining every part of it. They both moaned at the wonderful sensations and Asa felt the radiant heat coming off of his body warming her own.

Gabriel had undressed them both, allowing Asa to get under the covers before removing the last piece of cloth from her body. Asa avoided looking at him while he undressed, and when his hot body slipped beside her in the bed, she weaved her limbs around him. He turned them around so that he was on top and carefully opened her legs, situating himself between them.

That time the sensation for both of them was different and Asa felt she could rightly call it love making and not just sex. Gabriel was showing her respect and affection, and although neither of them said the words, there were feelings, hidden behind every caress and kiss they shared.

Asa suddenly realized she was day dreaming again and cursed under her breath. She really needed to get up and ready and get to work. She was already late as it was. Getting up quickly, she washed and dressed in a gray suit and black shirt, pulling her hair back into a severe bun. She was almost ready to leave the hotel room when her phone rang, and she hurried to answer it.

"Agent Clark," she said into the phone.

"Gibson here," Todd spoke through the phone. "The results from the horseshoe came in. You need to get over here."

"On my way," Asa replied and closed the phone. So, she was

back in the game. Sparing one last glance at the room, Asa once again went back to Gabriel's motel room.

There was something magical in the way his lips covered hers and possessed her whole being. She could say it was easy to resist him, but she would be lying to herself. His hands held her close and Asa could feel her heat rising. As her mind knew she should slow things down, her body had other ideas.

When he lifted his head to look into her eyes, Asa let him go and took a few steps back. Gabriel followed, trying to claim her lips again.

'Stop this now... we need to talk...'she pleaded with him, but the man cornered her against the wall and kissed her again.

This time the kiss went deeper, as his tongue entered her mouth and began to explore it. Asa felt his hands wander over her back, her buttocks, her thighs... as if he was trying to memorize every curve of her body.

Asa arrived at the FBI field office half an hour later. Ann had greeted her with a smile and a few of the others agents did the same, but Asa had no time to lose, and almost ran to Gibson's office. Agent Gibson was waiting for her and even stood up to welcome her.

"We have the results from the horseshoe analysis," he said with urgency in his voice. "The mark is consistent with a single shoemaker from Polson, Montana... near the Flathead Indian Reservation."

"That is great news," Asa replied. "Finally, a lead."

"We need to go and check it out," Gibson said, handing her the report to go through.

"Yeah, yeah," Asa said, too taken with the report to pay any attention to the man in the room. She was especially glad to have something to take her mind off the previous night and the man, who had so quickly taken over her thoughts.

Gibson watched her reading the report, moving to the door without even lifting her gaze from the paper.

"We'll take my car!" he told her as he closed door behind them.

Chapter 13

The agents arrived at a small town near Flathead Lake, Polson, just before lunch time and decided to get a bite to eat before meeting with the farrier who had made the horseshoe in question. They went into the first diner she saw on the way. Asa ordered a chicken salad with an ice tea, while Todd had a hamburger, fries, and a soda. They ate quickly and avoided unnecessary interaction with the locals.

Their meal finished, they loaded up and Asa drove to the feed store, which was the storefront for the barn, feed store, blacksmith shop and farrier. As they got out and looked around, Asa quickly realized she shouldn't have dressed in her suit for this trip. It screamed FBI, but it was too late now.

She walked around to the forge in the back and quickly found the stout-bellied farrier bent over a table and cleaning a horse shoe with a sharp instrument. Todd let Asa take the lead. A woman can often get a lot more out of a guy than another man can.

"Mr. Thomson?" she asked politely, and waited for the man to turn around. He was around fifty years old, with salt and pepper hair and a large moustache that made him look older.

"Yeah, that's me," he said, and started cleaning his hands with a rag. "How can I help you?"

"I am Agent Asa Clark with the FBI. This is Agent Gibson." She showed him her badge and walked closer. "We're here to ask you to look at some prints left by a horse."

The man looked at the pictures and compared them to the horseshoe in his hands.

"You are right about this being my work. That's definitely my mark. But I can't distinctively say who it belongs to. I sell a lot of these to ranches throughout Montana and even a few to neighboring states."

"Can you give me a list of the ranches who have bought

them?" Agent Clark asked, hoping for some other lead.

"Yes, I can probably do that, at least a partial list, but I'm not sure it will help you. A lot of these are purchased by wholesalers and stores. I sell very few of them direct," the man commented.

Asa thought about what he had said and saw the truth behind his words. "Thank you, anyway, Mr. Thomson. If you remember something, please don't hesitate to contact me," she added, and gave him a card with her phone number on it.

Mr. Thomson accepted the card, left the work he was doing and fired up a computer instead. He found and ran off a list of buyers, promising to call if something came to mind, but doubted that he would be of any help. She took the proffered list and thanked the man. She walked out of the barn, pondering her next move when a familiar face caught her attention. Gibson was still talking to the farrier.

At the feed store, which was situated just in front of the forge, she recognized Gabriel Kimble talking to two other men. She debated the wisdom of speaking to him. Although her mind was urging her to go, her heart wanted other things. Making it look like an accidental meeting, Asa walked towards Gabriel and his friends.

"Asa," he exclaimed, with a happy smile on his lips as he leaned down to kiss her on the cheek. She felt as if last night was replaying in front of her eyes and smiled back at him. "I wasn't expecting to see you so soon. And here of all places?"

"Yeah, it was a real surprise to me, too," The woman agreed and let him take her hand in his and turn her towards the other two men.

"Let me introduce you to my brother, David, and our neighbor, Ezekiel. Guys, this is Asa, we met yesterday at the pool hall in the city. She really showed some of the guys there how it's done."

"Nice to meet you, Miss..." David, Gabriel's brother said, extending his hand.

"Clark, Asa Clark," she said easily, accepting his hand. "It's nice to meet you, too."

The other man also offered his hand and then the two of them excused themselves and walked deeper into the store. Asa and Gabriel were left alone to talk and he surprised her by asking her for coffee and turning around without even waiting for an answer.

"You look very sure of yourself," she said playfully, and Gabriel had to stop and kiss her in the middle of the road, not caring who was watching them.

"Why are you complaining?" he asked, when he let go of her lips. "I thought that we agreed at least on that part of the situation?"

"You mean that we like each other?"

"Oh, you have no idea how much I like you," Gabriel said softly, managing to sound both passionate and gentle.

"Same here," Asa added, and they walked together into the café. She gave Gibson a quick call on the phone to say she was talking to someone and would see him in a little while.

"Tell me about your brother?" she asked, when they were all settled at a window table and had already ordered their coffee. "He looks a lot like you."

Gabriel looked out the window, as if searching for his brother and Asa could swear that she saw his eyes grow darker, as if he was scared.

"My brother," he repeated. "What can I tell you about my brother?"

Asa could tell that the atmosphere between them had changed. Gabriel was somehow guarded now, and had started to close in on himself. She didn't like it at all.

"Look, if you don't want to talk about him, don't. I was just curious."

"No, it's nothing like that." Gabriel smiled at her, some of the previous warmth returning to his gaze. "My brother is just a very sore subject to me. Since my parents died, he is everything to me and sometimes I feel a little trapped by him."

"That could be very painful," Asa agreed with him and waited to see if he was going to talk to her.

"David is ten years older than me, and as you could see, a very rustic type." Asa smiled at the memory of David's beard and his way of dressing. "He is the best cattle rancher in the area and a graduate of Montana State. He got his degree in modern ranching. His idea of happiness is living on the ranch with his family. My brother never dreamed of something more than that, and for that reason, it is apparently impossible for him to understand that I may want something more."

"So, this is the reason you looked so sad when I asked you about him?" Asa asked him. "I had a similar experience with my mother. She wanted to control every aspect of my life. I fought hard to finally earn the right to make decisions for myself, and after years of struggle, I was able to look her in the eye and say what I wanted."

"You're braver than me," Gabriel laughed, "I can see that already. Let's change the subject. Do you have plans for tonight?"

Before Asa could answer, David and Ezekiel walked past the coffee shop. Neither of them saw Gabriel and Asa inside, but Gabriel immediately became uneasy, causing Asa to take his hand in order to calm him down.

Asa watched the two men disappear inside another shop, and this time paid more attention to Ezekiel, who, at the moment, was carrying something very heavy in a simple bag. He was probably the same age as David and had a similar body build. The agent in her immediately wondered what he was carrying in that bag, but made the wise decision not to ask Gabriel about it.

By that time, Gabriel had recovered and was looking at her expectantly. "So, what do you say? Are you going to come to dinner with me tonight?"

"Tonight?" Asa was surprised by his invitation and at first was ready to refuse, but then she remembered the instructions from headquarters to get closer to the locals, so she decided that this would be a great chance to be seen with a local man. She hoped that the Kalispell population would open up to her based on her friendship with Gabriel.

"Okay, I don't have any plans for tonight. Oh, I didn't mean it that way. Sorry, I meant that I would be happy to have dinner with you."

Gabriel laughed at her confused speech and leaned across the table to give her another kiss.

"A yes would have sufficed, but your speech was also good," he teased, watching as Asa became a little red in the cheeks.

"Where should we meet?" she asked him. "I have to get going now."

"You surely saw the big cinema sign on the main street, right? At few feet from it is a small family restaurant, it serves the best food in the area. Meet me there?"

"Okay, I will meet you there," she promised, and with a final kiss, said goodbye for the moment, and went off to find Gibson, who was pretty irritated because she had disappeared with little explanation.

Chapter 14

Later that night, Asa dressed with care in a beautiful silk blouse and elegant skirt. She decided to wear her hair loose, put on some light makeup and walk to the restaurant, arriving just in time. She expected Gabriel to come in a car, but he surprised her once again by arriving on horseback. She watched him ride towards her on the back of a beautiful black horse.

Asa thought her heart skipped a few beats when she saw him for the first time. He looked magnificent on the back of the horse, dressed in a traditional jacket and a cowboy hat. The man approached her slowly and stopped the horse right in front of her, but Asa didn't move away. On the contrary, she stood her ground and even caressed the horse.

"Now, this was unexpected," she said to him with a smile. "Why didn't you tell me that you intended to arrive in such style? I could have done the same."

"You like riding?" Gabriel asked, surprised.

"I am half American Indian, don't you remember?" Asa asked playfully.

"Oh, believe me, I remember that part," he said, climbing down from the horse. "I changed my mind about where we're going for dinner. Do you mind?"

"No, not at all." Asa shook her head. "Where are you taking me?"

"This way, my lady." Gabriel pointed at a side street and they walked side by side, with the horse following them. After a few feet, Asa was surprised to see a large meadow and people dancing, eating and walking around. The place was like an oasis in amidst the buildings around it, and was obviously used for fairs and country gatherings.

"What is this?" Asa asked, and Gabriel laughed.

"This is the traditional restaurant of Uncle Bobby," he

exclaimed. "You will like it, of that I am certain."

Asa didn't disagree, as she already had thought the same. She followed him to a wooden table for two at the far end of the restaurant.

"This area is for more intimate gatherings. Oh, and I should warn you against the local chili. Don't try it."

They sat down at the table and the waitress came quickly by to serve them. Both of them ordered from the barbeque menu, together with a couple of beers. The horse was taken to a nearby stable.

"Tell me about your horse?" Asa asked. "It looks like a magnificent animal."

"Oh, he is magnificent, you can say that for sure," the man agreed proudly. "I've had him since he was only a year old. You could say that we grew up together."

"I always dreamed of having a horse, a dog or even just a cat, but my way of life never gave me the opportunity. I am really jealous of you right now."

"That must be one of the few perks of living on a cattle ranch," Gabriel laughed. "Personally, I am just glad that I'm not too far from town, because all of that close contact with nature can be a bit too much sometimes."

Asa had the time of her life, having a romantic dinner with Gabriel. She really wanted to get to know him better and the moment seemed perfect for that. They talked about each other's dreams and aspirations. Asa learned of Gabriel's great desire to get out of Montana and see the world, and Gabriel found it funny that Asa wished to see China, traveling to reach it by the sea. The only dark moment in the evening was Asa's failure to mention that she was an FBI agent in town on business. She still wasn't sure if he would accept the truth, and although she never actually spoke about her job to Gabriel at all, she still felt like she was lying to him.

"I am here to reconnect with my Salish Indian roots," she answered, when he asked about the reasons for her visit in Montana.

"Then you should come to the Kimble Ranch for a real taste of Montana life," Gabriel said, when the evening drew to a close.

"That would be great," she agreed. "But, not tomorrow. We could talk about it again and make arrangements, maybe in a day or so, okay?"

Asa could see that Gabriel Kimble was a kind-hearted, soft spoken young man who loved his family. He was a cattle rancher carrying on the family business, but he wanted more from life than Kalispell, Montana could offer. He wanted to see the world and embrace the diversity it had to offer.

After dinner, Gabriel took Asa to the back of the meadow, where a small stream was running through a beautiful forest.

"They try to keep nature as close to town as possible here," he explained.

They walked in silence through the woods, following the almost invisible paths, until they reached a secluded place with a bench under the trees.

With an easy rise of his right hand, Gabriel proceeded to wrap his arm around her waist. "What are you doing?" Asa asked, looking up at him. She was trembling, excited, and she was waiting for him to touch her, to show her what it meant to be loved by him. But, it was wrong, it was so wrong to do it out in the open, it hurt her to think about it.

He placed a gentle kiss on her forehead and then another on the exposed skin of her neck. His hands had wormed their way around her slender body and he was playing with her long hair.

"Let me go," Asa said in a loud whisper. "I don't think this is the right time or place for this." She was speaking the words with her mouth, but her body was leaning against him, having a mind of its own.

"Ha!" Gabriel exclaimed, "I think otherwise," he said, not fooled at all by her words.

"Why are you doing this?" she asked, exasperated.

"Because I hate it when people tell me what to do…"

"I'm not doing that," she insisted, but he didn't answer her that time, or at least not with words. Gabriel turned her slender body in his arms and claimed her lips in a searing kiss. In her surprise, Asa opened her mouth and he used her distraction to exploit the opportunity. His tongue explored her mouth, drinking from its sweetness, a sweetness he had never tasted before. Asa tried fighting the passion that was once again taking over her logical mind, but he never gave her the chance to step back.

Gabriel continued to kiss her, while lifting her skirt and removing her underwear. The soft piece of cloth fell on the ground unnoticed by Asa, whose mind was clouded by the adrenaline and passion running through her veins. He was moving quickly, not willing to lose any more time.

In his mind, this was a cure, something that was going to free him from his dull life. The man stepped back and lowered himself on the bench, bringing the woman down with him. If Asa was surprised to find herself straddling him, she had no time to show it, because Gabriel started sucking at her breast through the thin silk of her blouse.

"Oh," was all that came out of Asa's mouth.

Gabriel opened his pants and raised her up, so that she could sit on him. Asa closed her eyes, so that she could fully experience the feeling. His erection filled her so beautifully that she couldn't want anything more.

Gabriel wanted to undress her completely and explore every inch of her body with his hands and mouth, but this wasn't the place or the time for that. He had made sure to look around for other couples, aware that he couldn't risk Asa's reputation should someone come in their direction.

Asa was lying in his arms, leaving him to do all the work, but Gabriel didn't mind, on the contrary, it gave him a strange feeling of power to know that he was the one in charge. One of his hands was supporting her left hip, while the other had sneaked under her skirt and was caressing her burning hot skin, providing more pleasure.

The woman was touching only his shoulders, as if afraid to ruin his clothes. It made Gabriel regret not having more privacy. He was feeling at home inside this beautiful woman who was moaning against his neck and making him forget all the problems in the world. With a soft cry, Asa reached her orgasm and Gabriel waited for her to relax a little before making a dozen more thrusts and coming himself.

"We keep meeting and having sex," Asa heard the man speaking against her ear.

"Someone might come by…" Asa suddenly remembered and tried to get up, but Gabriel was holding her down with both of his hands, not allowing her to move even an inch.

"I didn't see anyone on the way here," Gabriel informed her calmly. "Now, tell me what you are thinking?"

"About what?"

"About what happened two days ago, and what is happening right now."

"What am I supposed to think? We had sex," Asa said softly.

"Just sex, Asa," Gabriel corrected her softly.

"Why, what would you call it?" Asa said, and finally lifted her head to look at him. The sudden movement not only put them eye to eye, but reminded both of them that they were still connected in the most intimate of ways.

"God!" she whispered and felt the heat rise in her face.

"What we have is special, Asa, you have to believe me." Gabriel smiled at her discomfort and adjusted their position so he could slide even deeper inside of her.

"I know that you may not see it, but there aren't many people that can say they had had what we shared just now."

"Really?" Asa asked again, and couldn't suppress a deep moan, caused primarily by Gabriel's movements inside her. "I think I believe you, as not too many people have sex in the forest."

Something moved in the forest behind Asa and interrupted their laughter. Both Asa and Gabriel let out a deep breath and carefully dislocated. The woman turned her back to the man and tried to adjust her clothes and underwear without showing too much. Gabriel, however, had none of her problems and adjusted his pants right in front of her. When they were both dressed and looking presentable, Gabriel approached her and carefully redid one of the buttons of her shirt. The action put his hand right over Asa's left breast, which was still wet from his kisses.

"You are an extraordinary woman, Asa. Never forget that," were Gabriel's last words before helping her up.

Chapter 15

Gabriel called her the next day and they arranged for Asa to drive to the Kimble's ranch the following weekend to meet him and his family. Asa was feeling a bit uneasy about not telling him the whole truth about herself, but she also realized that it could be very hard for Gabriel and his family to accept her as an FBI agent, especially before getting to know her. The young woman wanted to convince herself that was the only reason, but at the back of her mind, there was still the nagging feeling that there was more.

On Sunday, Agent Asa Clark drove to the Kimble Ranch. She was both excited about meeting Gabriel and worried what she might find there. The man had given her more than any other man she had known, but Asa still wasn't sure about her real feelings for the man, and had some niggling concerns.

The trip to the ranch wasn't long enough for her find answers to any of the questions that were bothering her. Asa enjoyed the ride and if it wasn't for her tortured mind, she might even say she was happy. The vast meadows, the green woods, and the beautiful scenery all reminded her of her childhood and the time she spent with her mother's family.

The FBI agent was surprised to see how big the Kimble Ranch was and had to take a deep breath before climbing down from the car. She had left behind all signs that she was an FBI agent and was dressed in a comfortable long skirt and a red cotton shirt. A nice pair of boots completed her look, and Asa really hoped that she would make a good first impression.

She walked towards the main building, looking around but seeing no one, at least not until an old man opened the door and walked outside. Asa froze as he brought a rifle outside, pointing it right at her.

"Grandpa, grandpa." It was Gabriel calling from one of the buildings on Asa's left, and running towards them. "This is Asa. I told you about her coming here this morning, remember?"

The young man ran over to the porch steps and gently lifted the gun from the old man's grasp.

"You really don't need this, now," Gabriel said, speaking calmly and putting the rifle down beside the door. Asa could tell that the old man still wasn't convinced, but he didn't make any attempt to protest.

"Asa, Hi!" Gabriel turned towards her laughing. "Let me introduce you to my Grandpa Joe. Grandpa, this is Asa."

The young woman could see how hard it was for the old man to let the younger man treat him like that, but he kept his mouth shut about it.

"Nice to meet you, young lady," he finally said. "And I am sorry for the old girl here," he said, pointing at his rifle. "It's never safe to meet new people."

"Nice to meet you too, Mr. Kimble." Asa smiled at him and walked up the stairs. "You have a really nice home, here."

"Call me, Grandpa Joe," the old man said. "Everybody calls me that."

"Okay, Grandpa Joe it is. You can call me, Asa," she said. "Thank you for inviting me here." She found Grandpa Joe to be quite adorable, and put her hands up.

"By the way, Mister, I am here to see your grandson, Gabriel."

The man in question watched the scene with amusement and let them play along. Grandpa Joe took the hint and pointed at her warningly.

"You make sure to take good care of my grandson—or else."

"Asa, excuse me for a minute," Gabriel suddenly said. "I need to take care of something, and I'll be back in just a few minutes."

Asa watched him go, when a big gray dog came out of the house through the still open door and started sniffing at Grandpa Joe's boots. The old man tried to send it away, but the dog acted like a puppy and refused to go away.

"Blue," he said to the dog. "Go away, boy." But the dog didn't move, and lay down beside his foot. Giving up on sending the dog away, Grandpa Joe looked back up at her and asked in a stern voice.

"Are you a Salish woman?"

"Yes, my mother is Salish." The young woman smiled at him, loving how the dog and the old man interacted.

"Good." He seemed pleased with the fact. "A long time ago, when my brothers were still alive, we used to meet with a few Salish girls, but their brothers weren't happy about it and never left us in peace. But, we were young and strong then, and it was just a game to us to chase them back to the reservation. One time, one of the boys was too much in love with one of the girls and we had to give him a lesson in how things are done in our world..."

"Grandpa." A young woman stepped out of the house and interrupted him. "Are you telling another one of your stupid stories?"

Asa had somehow felt hurt by the story told by the old man, but she decided not to show it. She understood how a man as old as Grandpa Joe might not understand what was in his stories.

"Please excuse the old man for his story, Miss," the young woman said to Asa. "My name is Jane Kimble, and we don't get many visitors out here."

"Asa, Asa Clark," she answered, and accepted her handshake. "I came here to see Gabriel."

"Come, I will take you to him," Jane said politely, and turned around, heading off the way Gabriel had disappeared just a few moments before.

"Gabriel seems like a great guy," Asa commented, while they walked towards the barn. "He must be a great help here."

"Asa!" Gabriel suddenly called, running towards them. "Sorry for leaving you alone for so long. I am sure Jane took good care of you."

"No problem." Asa smiled at him and accepted his kiss gratefully. "This place is amazing."

"Yes, it is," the man walking behind Gabriel said. "And you're right, my brother is a very great help in keeping it this way."

"David is just kidding," Gabriel pushed away the compliment. "We all work together for the success of the ranch."

Asa noticed that David and Ezekiel, their neighbor, were together again, and looked very grave. Gabriel also looked worried, although he tried to act as if everything was okay. He was holding her hand when he introduced her to everyone again.

"Listen," he turned towards her, after the others had go to the house. "Are you ready to saddle up?"

"Always." Asa smiled up at him and followed him to the stable. Gabriel gave her a beautiful light brown horse and they rode out across the vast property of the ranch. It was relaxing and exciting to Asa to ride in the open fields together with a man she was really starting to like.

Gabriel used the time they had together to tell her about the ranch, his family, and the way he wanted his future to be. Asa provided some narrative about the times she had been riding with her mother's family during the summers in and near the reservation, and she asked a few questions about how they took care of their cattle business.

Chapter 16

When they returned from the ride, it was almost time for dinner. Gabriel showed her a room where she could wash up and prepare for the meal. She didn't waste too much time getting ready and walked into the family's rustic dining hall only a few minutes later. Inside the room were Grandpa Joe, Gabriel, David and his wife Jane, all four of them busy doing something to set the table for dinner.

"Good evening," Asa said, walking in as they all turned to look at her. Gabriel quickly approached her and guided her to her seat.

They all sat down and once again Asa couldn't help but notice the way they were interacting with each other. It was as if the old man had been, yet still was the one with the power, but now the control was slowly being taken away from him by David, who looked very comfortable in his new role. His wife, Jane, also seemed comfortable with the situation, and acted as if she was the queen of some imaginary kingdom of hers. Gabriel, on the other hand, was completely out of his depth, and Asa could feel how out of place he was.

The conversation ranged across various topics of ranching, but also arguments around the way the government was working, though it seemed that David and Grandpa Joe were more 'old school' and wanted to fiercely protect their way of life, while Gabriel would rather have talked about more pleasant topics. Jane kept a largely superior silence as she presided over the meal. Asa disliked the woman, but kept her feelings under control and as she cared very little about politics, wished to change the subject and break the tension in the room. Asa could see that Gabriel wanted to bring her into his way of life and introduce her to his family.

"There are other things to talk about," he said at last.

"That's right," his brother said. "Leave the main things we

care about and talk about things that don't matter, instead." Gabriel protested that they had a guest and she didn't want to hear about ranching, but he was outnumbered by the rest of the family. It made her quite uncomfortable. There were other factors at play here, and at the moment, she could not figure out just what they were.

When the dinner was over and it was time for Asa to leave, Gabriel took her to the car and let her lean against it. "I am sorry for my family," the man said, leaning down to kiss her on the nose. "They mean well, but can be a bit too much sometimes."

"I don't mind," Asa smiled up at him. "Actually, I like the fact that they are so passionate about their beliefs. And I like them, too. Your grandfather is a real charmer. After meeting him, I understand where you get that smile of yours."

"Oh, you really know how to make a man feel special," Gabriel answered, and leaned down to kiss her on the lips, lightly at first, but then putting more passion into it. "You should stay."

"I would really like that," Asa agreed. "But, I have a lot to do back in the city and should really get going now."

"When will I see you again?" Gabriel asked, his lips still too close to hers for Asa to feel comfortable.

"Call me, and we can have another date," she offered.

"I would really like that," the man repeated her previous words. "I will call you soon. So, wait for my call."

With another long kiss, Asa said her goodbye and climbed into the car, heading back to the city with a happy smile on her lips. When she was far enough away and the spell Gabriel had put her under was somehow weakened, Asa started thinking about the last few days and the people she had gotten to know better.

David Kimble, Gabriel's brother, had turned out to be a simple man, who had been forced to take a leadership role with his family after the untimely death of his father. He was a gruff, humorless man, who was consumed by thoughts of duty, work and worry. His wife, Jane, was very much like him. Asa had noticed that David often talked about having a child, and thought that it really bothered him that he still hadn't had one. Jane was the one she did not like at all.

Grandpa Joe Kimble, on the other hand, was already seventy-one years old, and although he was old and frail, he still had the spirit of his old self. The man was very aware of the world at large and preferred to live in the close quarters of the ranch rather than face the rigors of that outside world. He had told Asa that his favorite way to pass the time was sitting on his front porch, cursing at invisible people and smoking his tobacco pipe. And yet, she had noticed that his grandchildren, and even their neighbor, Ezekiel Warren, saw the old man as a living icon of their way of life on the ranch.

Jane Kimble followed the example of the men in the family, and supported her husband in everything he was doing. Jane clearly was fearful that Asa was having too much influence on Gabriel and was distrustful of her. Jane had told Asa that she never wanted anything else from life. In her opinion, what she had now was more than enough for her. That all she wanted was a big happy family and to all live together on the ranch.

In these parts of the country, Asa knew that Jane's values and work ethic made her a positive example for all the ranchers and farmers. In some ways, she reminded Asa of her own mother and her mother's family.

Chapter 17

The next day, Asa Clark woke up running late, but couldn't seem to get out of bed. She was still under a spell from a beautiful dream she had been having of her and Gabriel together, making love. The images of the two of them rolling around on her bed were too powerful for Asa to forget so easily. She was really starting to fall for him, and for the first time in her life that thought wasn't scaring her.

So, that Monday morning, FBI agent Asa Clark arrived late for work at the FBI field office. No one seemed to notice, except Todd Gibson, who came out of his office and called to her in a sturdy voice.

"Agent Clark, could you come into my office for a moment?" he called.

Asa went in and closed the door.

"Sorry I'm late," she apologized. "Have we got some new information?" Gibson nodded and indicated a seat. He passed a report across the desk to her and asked if she had anything more to add. She shook her head.

"I did try and get closer to the locals and get a feel for the place." She took the report and Gibson told her what it contained.

"The lab turned up something from the missing agent's vehicle," he pointed out. "On the gas pedal, there was a distinct class of dirt which is found in the eastern part of Kalispell."

"That's good news," Asa said. "I was hoping that would happen and that we could use the results to find out which area they were investigating just before they went missing."

Agent Clark took the seat in front of his desk and started reading the information provided by the lab. According to them, the dirt had a specific construction, which placed it from a specific area of the country. It seemed that whoever had driven the car had transported the dirt inside on the gas pedal.

Both agents poured over the sediment samples and compared

them with the map of the region, which showed the different kinds of dirt found there. After half an hour, they managed to determine that the dirt was coming from a certain region. They were about to sort out which local police jurisdiction they should call for help, when Agent Gibson's phone rang.

Todd answered the phone, looking at Asa and silently asking her to give him a moment. "Gibson," he said into the phone. "Can you repeat that once more, please?"

Asa could tell that whatever news he was given was important. Todd stood up and looked concerned. "Okay, understood. We will be there as soon as possible," he told the caller, before terminating the call.

"That was a local police department," Gibson said to Asa. "Two unidentified bodies have turned up near Flathead Lake. They could very well be our agents. The area is right and according to the police they have been there for a while."

"No documents that can help us identify them?" she asked him, standing up too and walking towards the door. "I'll grab my jacket and be ready to go," she added

Clark took her jacket and slowly walked out of the FBI office, heading towards her car which was parked nearby. Gibson was still nowhere to be seen, so she had some time to gather her thoughts before they headed to the morgue.

Chapter 18

Taking his time to clear his own thoughts, Agent Gibson joined her in the car, and together they headed towards the Kalispell morgue. It wasn't a long drive, just a few blocks, but it was on both of their minds that these were most probably their missing agents.

In the morgue, the medical examiner, who had examined the bodies, came to talk to them immediately.

"Agents Gibson and Clark," Todd spoke for both of them. "Can you fill us in on your preliminary findings?"

"Agents, I'm Doctor Malow, I have done the initial assessment work on the two bodies," the young doctor introduced himself. "I still have a lot to do, full autopsies and formal identification, of course, but I can tell you what I have so far. The two bodies are badly decomposed, but my initial findings match the profiles of the two missing FBI agents, so I feel confident saying these are very likely the missing agents. I am sorry about that, by the way," the doctor added, looking up at the both of them.

"Another very interesting fact is that both bodies are filled with bullets. Whoever killed them was determined to make sure they were dead..."

Asa visibly shuddered at the news and saw how Gibson tried to hide his own discomfort behind a cough. The medical examiner showed them the photos of the bodies, insisting that it was better for them not to see the real bodies. The photos showed a heap of decomposed flesh, covered in blood and dirt. The carefully photographed bullet entries looked ominous against the dead flesh of the agents.

"From what I can see so far, the multiple bullet entries indicate well-trained shooters, yet not a single bullet hit the vehicle," Asa Clark pointed out. "That must mean something."

"That is interesting," the doctor commented. "But, maybe the two agents simply weren't in the car when they were killed?"

"There is no maybe about it." Asa picked up another photo and thought back to the photos of the two agents she had studied in the case file she'd been provided when she was assigned to the case. Two healthy young men ready to turn the world around for what they believed in. Now, here they were, dead, dumped in the wilderness, their decomposing bodies riddled with bullets; meanwhile their killers were still on the loose.

She still couldn't understand what was going on here, but one thing was for sure, it was serious business. Gibson demanded to see the personal effects of the agents, while Asa remained in the room with the photos and the medical examiner's preliminary report. She went through the whole thing repeatedly, until it became obvious that there was nothing new.

Cursing under her breath, Asa took out her phone and dialed the number in Salt Lake City, waiting for the Deputy Director to answer. On the third ring, Shepherd answered and Asa prepared herself for yet another hard conversation.

"Asa Clark here, Sir," she said, and continued. "Two badly decomposed bodies were discovered today, and they appear to be our agents. I'm sorry, Sir."

"Bodies… right." The Deputy Director sighed, "I don't know why, but I'd still hoped for a better result."

"Full autopsies are pending of course, but these men were shot multiple times, by multiple shooters," Clark continued. "M.E. says, they've been dead for more than a week, so it's safe to say they were probably killed the same day they disappeared."

"Yeah, that sounds about right," Shepherd commented. "Now you have something to work with, Agent. I hope you'll be able to find these men some justice soon."

"Yes, Sir," Agent Clark said readily. "We have the site where the bodies were dumped and the one where we found the car. That will help us to triangulate the possible position of the murder."

"Okay, okay," Shepherd agreed. "You do just that, but now Agent Clark, please explain to me just what is going on with you.

What's all this I'm hearing about your recent behavior?"

"What recent behavior is that, Sir?" Asa tried to act as if she had no idea what it was all about.

"Let me see." The Deputy Director didn't let her escape so easily. "According to Agent Gibson, you have been indulging in some... drinking with the locals. I know I told you to mingle, and while your willingness to follow orders is... admirable, I don't recall telling you to go quite so far."

"I'm not sure what Agent Gibson told you," Asa said coldly. "But, I haven't done anything to jeopardize the investigation, I can assure you. All I did was visit a pool hall and play some pool. I made a few friends among the locals and even was invited to one of the ranches around here. It all helps the case."

"Okay, okay," Josie Shepherd sighed into the phone at Clark's angry explanation. "I suppose Gibson may be a bit resentful about an outsider coming in to take over. Anyway, all I want is to see results from now on. Stop any other nonsense and do your job. You're a good agent, Clark, don't spoil it with this one."

Deputy Director Josie Shepherd ended the call and leaned back in her chair. She really needed to become more personally involved in the case. It was big and needed to be resolved quickly and well. And if agent Asa Clark wasn't able to do so, Shepherd was going to have to intervene herself. Her own bosses were waiting for the case to be concluded.

Back in Montana, Asa Clark was walking quickly out of the city morgue, looking determined. Gibson had already left the building and walked back to the FBI field office.

Chapter 19

With a renewed fervor for the case, Agent Clark decided to start visiting the outlying ranches and farms in the area. According to the scenario she and Gibson had hypothetically described, the agents were killed somewhere close to the city, probably at one of the farms or ranches they had been visiting. Asa had already seen firsthand how local farmers treated strangers and she could imagine what some fanatics could do if they thought the FBI was coming to look into their business.

The working theory was that a group of local crooks had managed to corner the two agents and kill them. Gibson was convinced that Smith and Holliday had managed to step on someone's toes and had gotten themselves killed. Asa wasn't so sure about that, and still wanted to think there might be some other explanation. *Drugs*, she thought. It definitely fit, and history proved that there was usually big money or drugs involved when people were murdered.

The next day, Asa filled her car tank with fuel and headed towards the nearest ranch in the area which Gibson had pointed to on a map. Asa really wanted to enjoy the trip in the country, but the different theories in her mind were too disturbing for her to really have a good time driving around.

At the first farm, Asa was greeted by a nice looking woman, who invited her inside and offered a cup of tea.

"I saw those two men, dear," Mrs. Keller said, while cutting her a piece of pie. "They spoke to my husband and he told me they had asked about anything unusual in the area."

"Can you tell me the exact time that happened?" Asa asked, and took another bite of the delicious pie.

"Yes, if I remember correctly, it happened around three weeks ago," Mrs. Keller said. "It was nearly lunch time and I ask them to stay for the meal, but they said they had too much work to do and were going to eat in the car. I had a nice roasted chicken that day and sweet potatoes, too. So, they climbed back in their car and went on to the next farm. They asked about it and my husband gave them directions on how to get there. I can do the same for you if you like?"

"That would be so great, Mrs. Keller, thank you," Asa said, with a big smile for the kind woman. "That pie was magnificent... the best. I don't think I've ever tasted pie that good before."

"Thank you, it's my mother's recipe. She left it to me," Mrs. Keller said proudly, and continued to chat happily.

Afterwards, she pointed the way to the next ranch and promised to call if anything else came to mind.

Agent Clark visited a few more farms and ranches, and was received differently by each owner. Most were nice, like Mrs. Keller. She noticed that a few of the ranchers refused to talk directly to her, although none of them told her to get off their property.

She made a point to ask each of them about the dead FBI officers and watched their reaction to her questions. Some of them said they hadn't seen them, while others affirmed that the agents did visit them and had asked them questions about the area. Asa questioned them about their answers to the agents and took notes of what they had said.

Clark noticed that she was getting closer to the Kimble's farm and that worried her. She hadn't been completely honest with them and the fact was making her uneasy. She didn't really care about the family's reaction, but Gabriel and his feelings were important to her. Unsure of what to do next, Asa decided to stay away from the Kimble farm for the time being, or at least until there was no other choice for her. And anyway, there were plenty more other places for her to visit without that complication.

One of the last ones she visited belonged to the man named Ezekiel Warren whom Asa remembered seeing at the Kimble's ranch. From the very beginning the man was tight-lipped, but she didn't give up.

"Can you tell me if two FBI agents came to your farm in the

last two weeks?" she asked politely.

"Who is asking?" the man asked in a cold voice.

"My name is Asa Clark, I am an FBI agent." She showed him her badge and waited for an answer.

"No, Agent Asa Clark." The man made sure to use her whole name. "I haven't seen those agents before." Ezekiel Warren pointed at the photographs of the two agents.

"Okay, Mr. Warren, thank you for your time," Clark said to him and walked back to her car. The man stood in the middle of the road leading to his house until the car disappeared from view.

Asa returned to the FBI field office later in the afternoon and sat behind her desk to go through her notes. She needed to compare everything she had found and try to find something that connected the ranches to the killing of the agents. She started slowly by tracing a diagram of the area in which the deceased agents conducted their study, and comparing them to her own field notes. The young FBI agent noticed there was a pattern in their notes. They seemed to have been on to something, but Asa just couldn't figure out just what it was yet.

Chapter 20

After another few days of hard investigating, Asa was exhausted and exasperated. No new leads had come to her attention and her own field trips weren't leading anywhere, a fact that made her wonder if she was the right person for the job. Asa had never felt that way about her work before and it made her think she should find something quickly if she wanted to keep her sanity.

Friday evening, she found herself walking towards the nearest local bar and ordering a drink. She sat at the bar alone and her somber expression warned the lonely men around her to keep away. Asa drank in silence for about twenty minutes, concerned that she wasn't making progress with the case.

As she finished her drink and spent another twenty minutes focused on reviewing her actions again trying to see what she was missing about this case. Asa was about to leave and go back to the hotel when she saw Gabriel, his brother and his sister-in-law entering the bar. She was horrified. She had been ignoring Gabriel's calls for nearly a week now, fearing she would have to explain her job and the reason she came here in the first place.

Asa considered leaving the bar unnoticed by the three of them, but Jane spotted her almost immediately and pointed her out to the others. The small group came towards her and Asa stood up to greet them.

"Asa, hello. We hadn't heard from you," Jane said, after they all shook hands and ordered something to drink. "Gabriel said you were too busy."

"Yes," Asa answered, embarrassed and irritated by Jane's negative choice of words. "Actually, I was about to call you..." Asa let her voice die down and made a point of looking right at Gabriel.

"I was wondering why I hadn't heard from you," Gabriel said, repeating almost the same words Jane had used.

"I think this would be a good time for us to go now," David

commented, tugging Jane towards one of the tables at the back of the restaurant. Asa and Gabriel watched them go and only then did he sit in the empty bar stool beside her.

"Is everything okay?" Gabriel asked softly. "I thought there was something happening between us?"

"Yes and yes," Asa said quickly. "I'm sorry for not calling you; I think I was a bit afraid that things were happening too quickly between us."

"I can understand that," Gabriel smiled, and Asa realized how much she had missed that smile. "But now that fate has brought us back together, what would you say about starting anew?"

"Starting what anew?" Asa asked playfully.

"That thing that we might have had, but are still not sure about the speed of," Gabriel said, and both of them laughed at his rather confused expression.

Gabriel ordered them a round of drinks and they spoke about their previous meetings and the visit to the Kimble Ranch. Asa felt herself relax and wasn't surprised at all when she was laughing with him and leaning against his muscular body, all thoughts about her job, and the warnings from Gibson and Shepherd long forgotten.

"There was too much work at the farm these last days," Gabriel was saying. "But I couldn't stop thinking about you."

"Is that so?" The young woman smiled seductively and opened her bag to search for a tissue. "I wanted to ask you something."

She suddenly changed the tone, as her eyes fell on the photos of the two deceased agents.

"Have you heard anything about some dead FBI agents who were poking around in the area?"

"What?" Gabriel asked, surprised. "Dead FBI agents? I don't know. Why are you asking?"

"I heard someone talking about their bodies being found near the lake and wondered if you knew something more about it," Asa explained.

"Sorry, I don't know anything about it," he said, as he shook his head. "But, I know the lake is a wonderful place for a swim in the summer," he added playfully.

For another hour, they talked, drank, and kissed each other, until neither of them could take it anymore and Gabriel asked if she wanted to show him her hotel room. Asa didn't hesitate and agreed to show him, if he gave her two minutes to visit the ladies room first. Gabriel sent her away with a kiss and went to speak to his family.

"Don't wait for me," Gabriel told them with a secretive smile on his lips. "I may spend the night in town."

"So, you and Asa made up?" David asked in a rather cold tone of voice, while Jane excused herself and walked towards the bathroom.

Asa was washing her hands when Jane entered the bathroom and looked at the stalls, making sure that no one else was inside.

"Hi again," Jane said and leaned against the door. "I heard that you've been asking questions around town and in the outer areas?"

"Yeah?" Asa asked calmly, wishing that she wasn't so drunk right now. "What about it?"

"I don't know," Jane nodded slowly. "I was wondering if you are working for the Feds."

"I might be a very curious woman, but that doesn't make me an FBI agent. But, if I was one, I don't see how that changes anything," Asa tried to assure her.

"If you say so," Jane said, and walked out of the bathroom, still unsure what to think about it.

Twenty minutes later, Gabriel followed Asa's movements around the hotel room. Shit! The girl was really beautiful.

"Have to admit that you work very well under pressure," the man pointed out. He let his hands fall back and then stood up and moved around behind Asa. He leaned in close and breathed in her ear, "Don't you think that it will be much more fun, if you let me kiss you?"

"What makes you think that I want to kiss you?" Asa asked in a low voice.

"Let's see," he mused. "First, you cannot take your eyes off me." He counted, raising one of his fingers. "Second, you keep looking at my lips. Third, you just want to kiss me."

"Two of your points are about looking at you. Couldn't you find something more original?"

His breath was skimming across her skin, sending shivers down her back. Asa's breath hitched, while her lips burned with anticipation for that kiss. Swallowing, she looked up, watching Gabriel from under her lashes.

"Don't you have anything to say?"

"No, not really," the man said, his voice husky with barely concealed need.

"You repeat yourself."

Gabriel smiled, showing that he didn't really care who was going to win, and enjoying how much he was able to distract Asa, by just looking at her.

"Okay," she finally gave up. "And anyway, I don't really like playing games that much."

She smiled at his surprise, just before she turned around and kissed him on the lips. The kiss was both soft and firm, keeping her arms away from his body with only their mouths touching. Asa was shy and careful, but the Gabriel didn't have the same problem. He quickly caught up with the situation and ran his tongue across her lips, boldly asking for entrance.

Asa hesitated for a moment, then opened her mouth to let him in.

She could taste the alcohol he drank earlier. He leaned forward and jumped on her side of the sofa, immediately wrapping his hands around her slim waist, then gently caressing her back. He sighed at the feeling of his hands exploring her body, as their tongues gently caressed each other. A soft groan sounded in the hotel room, when Asa leaned closer to him and placed her arms around his neck.

The sound drew a quick response from her, making Asa open her mouth even more and letting Gabriel deepen the kiss. It was madness, but from the moment she set eyes on him, she felt as if it was all a dream. And when you dream, you allow yourself to do things you never do in real life, right? She was afraid, expecting at any moment to wake from her dream, so she did the only possible thing. She decided to savor every moment she was given with him. She already knew she would never forget this night, and the man who was kissing her with such abandon.

Gabriel felt her capitulation and proceeded to kiss her more possessively, hungrily, aggressively. She was someone he hadn't expected to want, hadn't wanted to meet, and yet, couldn't keep his hands off. One thing was for sure, he didn't want to stop holding her.

The new sensation drew a deep moan from Asa, her heart pounding so hard she wasn't able to hear anything else. His hands never seemed to cease skittering across her skin, making her blood rush through her veins and inflaming her body.

"Are you sure you don't want to taste my pie?" the man asked with his lips barely leaving hers.

"Later…" the woman whispered between ragged breaths.

That single word was enough for Gabriel to spring into action. He hooked his hands under her knees and shoulders and carried her closer to the bed. The light coming from the windows was throwing shadows over them and only the walls, creating beautiful pictures.

He kissed her again and slowly removed her shirt, and debated taking off her jeans. Asa didn't stop him which encouraged him even more so he did it, leaving her standing in just her underwear.

"Your turn," she said boldly, although her hands shook when she tried to undress him.

"Let me help," he replied, sliding his hand down her back and over her bottom.

It took a lot for him to let go of here and get undressed, never really looking anywhere else but at her. Then he was kissing her again, until they both ran out of breath and he lifted his face and looked at hers. Asa's cheeks were flushed and her lips swollen, but she was smiling, so everything was okay.

Gabriel wasn't used to dealing with women like her. Usually the women in his bed were local girls. Gabriel was tired of all those other women, they only wanted his money and never really cared about him. Nothing like the confident, beautiful Asa.

"We should wash and get dressed," Gabriel whispered, unwilling to end the moment.

Asa silently agreed and followed him to the small hotel bathroom. They washed each other silently, continuing to explore the other's bodies, but this time without the sexual heat from before. Gabriel acted the perfect gentleman and helped her out of the shower and wrapped her in a clean towel.

In the bedroom, he watched her dress in clean underwear and a shirt. During that time, the man was only covered with a towel around his hips, hiding nothing of his gorgeous body.

Asa returned to the bed, leaving Gabriel alone to finish dressing himself. She expected to feel uneasy and maybe even ashamed of what she had just done, but nothing of the kind occurred. On the contrary, Asa felt alive and full of joy, wishing only to relive the moment again and again.

Gabriel came out of the bathroom and with the coffee maker on the counter, put on the small pot of coffee. In no time, it was ready and he carried two cups over to the bed, offering one to Asa.

"Thank you." She smiled at him and sipped from the steaming cup.

The man sat down beside her and ran his hand over her knee. "It was amazing," Gabriel said softly. "You are amazing…"

Asa raised her vulnerable eyes to look at him and said nothing, preferring to lean her head on his shoulder and arrange her legs so they were off the floor.

"I have never felt this way," she confessed after a while.

"Okay," Gabriel confirmed. "But, it wasn't just me. You were the one who made all this so amazing. You inspired me."

Asa turned her head and placed a slow, wonderful kiss on his lips. The man's satisfied sigh said more than all the words in the world and Asa moved back to her previous place. "I always dreamed of meeting Prince Charming," she said in an ironic tone. "But, I never thought of actually meeting him."

Gabriel laughed softly and kissed her on the top of the head. "So, are you saying that I'm Prince Charming?"

"Yes, you don't believe me, but you will if you look at it as I do," Asa said seriously.

"You most certainly know how to turn things around so that they work for you." He worked his hand around her and let it lie on her stomach. "But, I very much doubt that the rest of the women will agree with your description of the prince."

"Oh, but we women are very practical," Asa disagreed with him. "We all know that the perfect Prince Charming is different for each of us."

The rest of the night, Asa and Gabriel talked a lot, laughing at each other's jokes and using every possible opportunity to touch and kiss. They talked a lot, but still managed to avoid everything related to the outside world. Gabriel told her about his dreams to change his life and become a better person, while Asa confided in him that she missed her family and wanted everything to be as before. They continued to sit on the comfortable bed, changing their position from time to time and kissing with renewed candor.

Gabriel left the hotel room in the early hours of the morning, leaving Asa asleep in the bed.

Chapter 21

Asa woke up in the morning and immediately turned over to find the bed empty and cold. She felt disappointed, but quickly let the feeling go, especially when she saw that there was a message waiting for her on her phone. Gabriel had left her a sweet message about seeing her later that same day and Asa smiled the whole time she washed, dressed and ran down the stairs.

The world looked amazing to her that morning and Asa smiled at the people she met at the diner and on the way to the office. She reported to the FBI field office just in time, but was surprised to find it almost deserted. Agent Gibson's office was empty and most of the desks were also missing their occupants. The woman on the front desk was busy talking on the phone with someone, who sounded like one of those fanatics who saw something bad in everything, so Asa went to look for someone else to talk to.

Ann was sitting behind her desk going through some paperwork, but as soon as she saw Asa, she jumped up and gestured for her to follow her into Gibson's empty office.

"Where is everyone?" Asa asked, when Ann closed the door behind her. "Is something going on?"

"You have no idea," Ann said, excited. "Agent Gibson went to the airport, because some high level agent from Salt Lake City is coming to town," Ann said in a loud whisper. "One of the analysts told me that it had to do with your case. According to him, the bosses weren't happy with how the case had been handled and are coming down here to shake things up."

"Do you know who it is that's coming?" Asa asked, already suspecting who it might be.

"I'm not sure, but it must be someone big, because Gibson almost ran out to meet him," Ann commented. "I thought that he called you, by the way?"

"No, but it's okay, we'll see who it is soon enough." Asa tried to hide her displeasure and worry about the situation. With a final thank you, she walked out of the FBI office, just in time to see Todd's vehicle pulling up. Beside him sat Deputy Director Josie Shepherd, looking very business-like, and probably here to oversee the investigation and keep a closer eye on her.

"Shit," Asa said, and waited for them to get out and come closer. The Deputy Director spotted her almost immediately, while Gibson took his time closing the car and putting up the windows.

"Agent Clark," the Deputy Director greeted her.

"Deputy Director," Asa answered and stepped aside, so that the other woman could walk inside. Clark spared a last glance to Gibson, telling him silently what she thought about him, then followed Shepherd inside.

The Deputy Director had already walked into Gibson's office and was sitting behind his desk, when Clark, followed closely by Gibson, entered the room and closed the door. Shepherd looked at them both and nodded for them to sit down.

"So, what can you tell me about this case of ours?" she asked no one in particular.

"I'm sure that Agent Gibson has been keeping you well informed, sir," Asa said.

She cleared her throat and for a few moments she remained silent. The she began, shifting her position in the chair opposite the Deputy Director.

"I have been following the steps of agents Smith and Holliday, during the last few days I visited most of the farms in the area and talked with the owners. Most of them confirmed that they had been visited by the two agents, while others say that they never came to their farm or ranch."

"What information were you able to gather?" the Deputy Director asked.

"There is a pattern in what the two agents were following," Agent Clark explained. "But, I'm still unsure what it is. It seems that they have been visiting certain places, while avoiding others. I'm not sure which of them were those under suspicion, the ones they visited or the ones they didn't."

"That is solid footwork," Shepherd said, "Is there anything else you can add?"

"I have found a lead based on the soil samples we recovered from the foot pedals of their car," Agent Gibson quickly stepped in. "I've been going around taking soil samples. According to the lab, the closest sample of dirt to that particular soil type is found near the Kimble Ranch."

"What else, Agent Gibson?" Shepherd asked the man.

"Agent Clark has been spending some time with one of the Kimble brothers," Gibson said carefully.

"Okay. Agent Clark, you will continue seeing this man. Let's see what you can find out about his ranch and family. Agent Gibson, you will help her and will report to me every step either of the two of you take. Now, Agent Gibson, will you excuse us? I need to speak to Agent Clark in private."

Gibson exited his own office without another word and Asa was left to face the Deputy Director alone. Shepherd didn't speak for a long moment, watching Asa in her chair.

"How did this happen, Clark?" she asked directly.

"I met him in a bar, and it was well before I was aware his ranch might be connected to the case," she answered honestly.

"What now?" Shepherd looked angry, the warning clear in her stance.

"Now, I will use him to gain the information we need to solve the murder of the two agents." Asa answered with what the Deputy Director was expecting her to say.

"Fine, now get back to work."

Chapter 22

At the same time, just outside the FBI office, David Kimble had watched Todd Gibson leave the building and walk back to his truck. David had already witnessed the arrival of the man together with a woman, as well as their short conversation with Asa Clark. The girl his brother was falling in love with had acted as if the woman was someone of importance, and by the looks of it, Todd Gibson was taking orders from her.

David Kimble had come to town for supplies and it was by pure chance that he passed in front of the FBI office and recognized Asa Clark. Feeling betrayed, the man climbed back into his truck and headed towards his ranch. There were things he needed to do, and preparations he needed to make.

Back at the Kimble Ranch, Gabriel was working in the barn while Jane prepared lunch. David arrived just in time to see his brother looking at the horizon, head in the clouds, obviously dreaming about something. The older brother could just imagine who Gabriel was dreaming about, and that only made him angrier.

"Gabriel," he called from the veranda. "Could you come in? I need to talk to you."

Gabriel walked back to the house quickly, thinking it must be something important for his brother to call him so urgently. He was still smiling when he stepped inside the kitchen, where he found his brother and Jane sitting on the table.

"What is it?" Gabriel asked, looking from one to the other. "Did something happen in town?"

"Sit down, Gabriel. We need to talk." David used a fatherly tone of voice and gestured to a chair in front of both of them.

"Why do I feel like I'm being judged?" the young man tried to joke.

"Listen, we need you to stop seeing that Clark woman," Jane spoke before her husband and then went silent.

"Gabriel," David started again. "We have been watching her closely and we know for sure now that she is an FBI agent."

"So what?" Gabriel asked defensively. "Is it a crime to be an FBI agent now?" Gabriel realized that this urgent meeting was them confronting him about his relationship and it made him angry.

"Asa is not the one for you," David responded.

"So, you've been following my girlfriend?" Gabriel asked them, a bit surprised. "What, were you worried about me or something?"

"You know how I feel, what with our business endeavors, Gabriel," David answered him. "An FBI agent has no place at our table or in our lives. You need to stop seeing her, immediately."

Gabriel loved and respected his brother, but not even David had the authority to tell him who to date. On the other hand, he also felt betrayed. Asa had obviously been using him to get closer to the locals, successfully hiding her real profession. When Gabriel thought about it, he realized that Asa had never actually told him just what she was working on, but he had also never asked her about it directly.

"I very well may stop seeing her, David, but not because of the reasons you gave," the younger man said. "I may stop seeing her because she wasn't honest with me and there is nothing that I hate more than someone lying to me, even by omission."

"That's right, good for you, Gabriel." Jane smiled at him and took his hand in hers. "From the first moment I saw her, I knew there was something fishy about her. Don't let women like Asa make you think that you should leave the people who have loved and cared for you your whole life. We are your family and we will always take care of you."

"Thank you, I know that Jane," Gabriel answered her sadly.

David watched him carefully and noticed how his brother fought the tears back. "I have a big job for you now and I need you to focus on it."

"What is it?"

"I have to go away for a while and I need you to take care of the ranch for me until I come back," David said gravely. "This is very important to all of us, which is why I want you to focus on our family and on the ranch."

"You're leaving and expect me to take care of everything by myself?" Gabriel asked, incredulous.

"Yes."

"But David, where are you going? Is there a problem? You know you can tell me anything, right?" Gabriel asked urgently.

"No, no, everything is okay." David smiled reassuringly. "I just need to do something and will be away for a while, that's all." In his mind, David was picturing the marijuana field so close to harvest. After that they'd be done with the cartels and the ranch would be saved. *If anybody was ever truly done once they had business with the cartel,* David thought.

"But..." Gabriel tried again.

"Please, Gabriel, just trust me on this? I can't tell you anything more for now, just that I will be on a cattle run up in the mountains," David pleaded with him, while Jane nodded encouragingly. "You just promise me that you will take care of Grandpa Joe."

Gabriel had a lot of other questions to ask, but the look on David's face told him that the subject was closed.

"Okay, I'll take care of Grandpa, of the ranch and of whatever else you need me to, but just promise me that everything is going to be okay?"

"Everything is going to be fine, I promise," David assured him. "Now, is dinner ready? Jane?"

Gabriel went to look for Grandpa Joe. Asa and what he felt for her was still on his mind. Gabriel did his best to forget about her, but it was too soon and too fast to forget someone as spectacular as Asa Clark.

Chapter 23

The next day, Agent Todd Gibson and Agent Asa Clark made their way to the Kimble Ranch in force. The orders had been clear and Asa hadn't wasted any more time considering her personal feelings. Gabriel had been a beautiful dream, but if the man turned out to be a criminal, Asa was going to put him behind bars and never think about him again. During the drive to the Kimble Ranch, she had lost herself in thoughts about the man and the few hours they had spent together.

Thankfully, Gibson had given her the time to rethink the whole situation and had spoken only once to warn her against getting involved with people she knew nothing about.

"Didn't I already make it clear that you should keep your thoughts to yourself?" She had been pretty short with him so Gibson had kept quiet after that.

They arrived at the ranch mid-morning and Grandpa Joe greeted them in his customary way with his rifle.

"Stop where you are, turn around and leave my property," the old man had shouted, pointing the old rifle at them.

Asa recognized the threat and acted quickly. She climbed out of the car and with raised hands and approached the porch.

"Grandpa Joe," she called at him. "It's me, Asa. I came here with Gabriel. Don't you remember me?"

"Asa?" the old man repeated. "The Salish girl? Yes, I remember. What do you want?"

"I want to talk to your grandsons," Asa answered, slowly approaching him. "Can you tell me who is home?"

"Gabriel is here," Grandpa Joe answered, lowering the rifle and taking out the pipe he had in his mouth. "What do you want with him?"

"I need to ask him a few questions. Can you call him for me?"

Grandpa Joe still looked suspiciously at her and Agent

Gibson, but after a few more seconds, he turned around and opened the door.

"Gabriel, come out boy," he called in a rugged voice and slowly lowered himself onto the bench beside the door.

"What is it Grandpa?" Asa heard Gabriel asking from inside. "Do you need something?"

Gabriel stepped out of the house and froze in place. His eyes were glued to Asa and she could read the hurt in them.

"Gabriel Kimble," she spoke. "My name is Agent Asa Clark and I am here to ask you a few questions about the death of two FBI agents."

"Agent Asa Clark," the man repeated. "Why did you lie to me about who you were?"

"Mr. Kimble, do you know something about the murdered agents?" As Asa asked the questions, her voice and behavior were strictly business. "And can you tell me where your brother is?"

"I told you already, I don't know anything about the murdered agents," Gabriel said, almost shouting. "And about my brother... my brother is in the mountain country on a cattle run. As you can see here, the pastures are drying up from the summer heat, and along with some of the other local ranchers, we moved our herds further north."

"And you really don't know anything about the missing agents?" This time it was Gibson, who asked the question.

"No, I have never seen them," Gabriel insisted.

"What about your brother, do you know if he knows something about them?" The FBI agents continued the investigation. Gabriel continued to answer no to all of their questions and Asa could see that he was telling the truth.

And then suddenly something unexpected happened.

"I sent those agents packing," Grandpa Joe commented with satisfaction.

"What are you talking about, Grandpa?" Gabriel asked him, surprised. "Did they come here?"

"Excuse me, Mr. Kimble, but we'll conduct the investigation." Gibson took the lead again. "What do you mean, you sent them packing?"

"I told them to get off of my property and went inside to get my rifle. When I came back out they were gone, probably scared for their lives."

"When did that happen, Grandpa Joe?" Asa asked.

"I can't exactly recall, but it surely was a few weeks back." The old man nodded to himself and put some more tobacco into his pipe.

It was obvious they weren't going to get anything more from him, so Asa Clark produced the search warrant they had and gave it to Gabriel.

"We have a search warrant allowing us to search the entire ranch," she said to him, looking pleadingly into his eyes.

"Go ahead, search everywhere," he told her. "I don't care."

Agent Gibson proceeded to search the property, and sent the team of police, deputies and agents they had brought along to do the same. They fanned out over all the property, looking for any evidence linking the Kimble family or ranch to the murder of the two field agents. Asa waited for them to put some distance between her and Gabriel, and then climbed up the stairs of the porch.

"Gabriel, I want to explain," Asa said, in a soft voice. "I didn't want to lie to you, but you never asked me directly and I just decided to omit the truth for the time being. It never occurred to me that your family might be involved."

"Omit the truth? Don't you understand that is the worst kind of lie there is, Agent Clark? " Gabriel asked, while the FBI agents were busy searching the property. " You had all the opportunity in the world to tell me the truth and you never did. Do you have any idea how I feel about you coming to my home, meeting my family, and all the while you were investigating your murder case?"

"I can imagine, but as I said, I never really suspected your family…"

"I don't want to hear it, Asa, I really don't," Gabriel said, then turned around to go back into the house.

"Gabriel, wait," Asa called after him and tried to reach out for his hand, but he just shook it off and closed the door in her face.

Asa felt humiliated, although she understood why he was acting like that. In his place, she would have done something much worse than closing a door.

Chapter 24

Asa didn't see Gabriel again after he closed the front door in her face, but she could tell that he was standing behind the windows, watching her. The search of the ranch continued for about two hours, but they found very little evidence that something horrible had happened on the grounds. One of the policemen found a few bullet entries on the walls of the buildings, as well as a few bullet casings on the ground, but there was no telling when the shots were fired. They collected the casings. They could be matched to, or excluded from, the bullets found in the bodies.

Agent Gibson insisted they look around one more time just to make sure there wasn't anything they could have missed. When it became obvious that they weren't going to find anything useful, Agent Clark gave the signal to pack up and go. She and Gibson were the last to load up.

Asa looked back at the house, searching for the man she had started to love.

"Come on, Clark," Gibson called from inside the car. "It is time to get back to Kalispell."

Asa climbed in and closed the door with slam, shaking the entire car. Gibson huffed at her antics, but didn't say anything. They drove in silence for a long time, until the man decided that she had calmed down enough.

Gibson just started talking about whatever came to mind as they drove. He was trying to distract her from the personal side of what had just happened at the ranch.

The woman listened to him, but didn't say anything. She wasn't in the mood for talking and the subject wasn't her favorite one either. Gibson and his problems didn't really interest her, but she had to admit that it took balls to say that he was sorry to a young woman like her.

"You saw the situation out here," Gibson continued. "We are

right in the middle of nowhere, and the big bosses tend to forget about our existence. We have very few interesting cases and when something really big comes our way, they send someone from the big city to work on it. You understand how that might get us irritated?"

"Yes, I understand." Asa sighed, thinking that she should cut him some slack. "Don't worry, we're okay, you were only doing your job."

"Yeah, well." Gibson looked ashamed. "Getting the attention of the Deputy Director is not a small thing. Especially when she was the one who sent you down here in the first place. She must really think a lot of you, because she refused to believe me for a long time."

"If you say so," Asa laughed sarcastically. "From my point of view, things look pretty different."

"I thought that you were stuck and needed an extra push," he said, finally and defensively.

By the time they finished their difficult conversation, they were on the outskirts of Kalispell. The town was very much alive at that hour of the day and they drove slowly towards the FBI field office. The rest of the cars were following them, and together the FBI vehicles entered the parking lot across the street from the bank building. Asa was about the open the car door, when suddenly a large explosion ripped through the building. Everyone around them ducked for cover as the entire building went up in a ball of flames.

Asa watched the flames eating the building out of the car window. A number of people were lying on the ground, hurt by the explosion and Asa finally moved from her safe place. She ran from one person to another, she was glad that although they were hurt, no one was dead. She could hear sirens coming their way and saw other agents coming forward to help with the injured. Gibson was the first to approach the bank building, but there was no going inside.

"God," Asa heard him say. "They're all dead."

She realized then that the bomb had most likely killed everyone inside the bank building. Covered in smut and breathing with difficulty, Asa tugged him back, afraid that he might get hurt by the falling debris. By that time the firefighters and the first ambulance had arrived, they were carrying away the injured and trying to find a way to enter the building.

"Can you see if there is anyone still alive inside?" Gibson asked one of the firefighters.

"Sorry, Todd, but no one could have survived that hell," the man answered, and together with one of his colleagues, started establishing the perimeter.

Asa stood behind the police line and watched the FBI building slowly disappear in the hungry flames. The firefighters had managed to enter the first floor and bring out three badly burned bodies of those who had been in the bank itself. Asa shivered at the sight of the dead bodies. Her only thought was that it could have been all of them in there. If they had arrived only a few minutes earlier, she, Gibson and everyone else would have also been dead.

"Agent Clark," Gibson spoke from her left side. "Deputy Director Shepherd is nowhere to be found." He gave her a few moments to process the news and then continued, "It is now up to us to find the people who did this."

"Yes, you're right, of course." Asa nodded, fighting back tears. "Do you know if Ann was inside?"

"No idea. Sorry, I just—" Gibson shook his head, as if to clear it. "Look, we have to find a place where we can quickly set up our office. We need space where we can examine the debris and see what it can tell us."

"Do you have something in mind?"

Asa never moved her eyes from the burning building. The firefighters had given up trying to stop the fire, instead, focusing on keeping the nearby buildings safe. She could tell that everything would be over soon. She was really afraid of what they were going to find. The big question in her mind was how many people had been inside the building at the time of the explosion. And who did this? Who planted a bomb inside a building full of innocent people?

"I was thinking about the building at the end of the street,"

Gibson answered, after what seemed like ages. "The place is empty at the moment and it's big enough for us to work out of."

Asa agreed silently and raised a hand to move the hair out of her eyes, only to realize that her hand was black and covered in blood.

Chapter 25

"Twenty-one people, among them, FBI Deputy Director Josie Shepherd, were killed in an explosion and ensuing fire in the bank building that also housed the FBI field office in Kalispell. According to experts, the bomb was planted inside the building. The explosion occurred in the early hours of the afternoon, taking everyone by surprise."

"Flames engulfed the exterior of the bank building within a matter of seconds, tearing through the building like paper." The news reporter from one of the local channels was speaking in an urgent and soulful voice, reiterating the terrible news to the people.

Everyone passing by could see FBI agents and various specialists systematically digging through the rubble left after the fire. The news channels were showing the agents carrying away pieces of wood, half burned files, equipment and other things; moving them to the new makeshift office, set up in a nearby building. However, that was the extent of what they could see, because the security at the new office was very tight, and no one was allowed to come near it.

Almost twenty-four hours later, the situation was just as critical. The Deputy Director was among the dead and a dozen other federal agents were now confirmed to have been killed in the blast. The FBI agents working the scene were shell-shocked, but determined to find out who was responsible for this attack, and for the murders of Agents Holliday and Smith.

The first thing they did was secure and set up office space, then they started pouring over the debris right away, bringing everything inside for testing and analysis. More agents and analysts arrived from the nearby FBI offices. Clark and Gibson were grateful for the help. This was not the time to feel threatened by someone coming in to assist. Everyone was giving the best of themselves to solve the case.

By the end of the first day after the blast, it became obvious that the bomb used for the attack was of a homemade variety, built by amateurs. That only served to confirm the theory that there was a cartel related organization in the area.

Knowing it was the only solid lead they had, Agent Todd Gibson ordered material witness warrants of every member of the Kimble family and named them as material witnesses.

The agents sent by Gibson to serve the warrants returned with only two members of the family. Asa watched Gabriel and Joe Kimble climb out of the car. "Where are the rest of them?" she asked one of the arresting agents.

"These two were the only ones on the ranch," the man explained. "It seems that no one has come in to the ranch since you left it yesterday."

"Did they resist when they were brought in?" She asked the question that had been bothering her from the very beginning.

"No, the young man came willingly and encouraged the older one to do the same," the agent explained.

"Okay, thank you," Asa dismissed him and walked into the area designed for interrogation. Gabriel and Grandpa Joe were sitting on two chairs.

"Come on, Asa, it's time to talk to them," Gibson spoke from behind her and startled her a little.

"Yeah," she agreed, took a deep breath and walked closer to the two arrested men.

Gibson and Asa sat down in front of Gabriel and Grandpa Joe, as the woman tried to catch Gabriel's eyes. She expected him to look away, but the young man looked straight at her and even smiled a little.

"I am sorry for what happened here," he said to her, looking sincere, and Asa believed him.

"Thank you," she answered, but Gibson cleared his throat and took the lead.

"Mr. Kimble, I suppose you know why you are here?" He

went right to the point.

"Yes," Gabriel answered, without any anger in his voice. "You think that I and my family know who is responsible for what happened to the missing FBI agents."

"And do you?" Gibson wasn't going to let the other man manipulate him into sympathy.

"No," Gabriel answered calmly again. "I know nothing about them. Or about the bombing if you want to ask me about that as well."

"What about your brother?" Asa joined the interrogation. "Could he be involved?"

"No..." This time Gabriel sounded worried. "My brother is up in the mountains. He's taking care of the cattle, like I already told you. He would never do something like that."

Asa noticed that only in his last sentence had Gabriel said that his brother was incapable of killing someone. It looked as if he was trying to convince himself that his brother was away, so it would be physically impossible for him to be in two places at once. Clark could tell that Gibson had noticed it too, and was on it like a dog with a bone.

"Do you know if your brother has any problems with banks?" Asa asked. It was something she had found in the notes from Agents Holliday and Smith. The Kimble's ranch was in foreclosure.

"Yes, my brother had some financial issues, but I cannot imagine him doing something like that," Gabriel answered.

"Have you ever heard anything about a criminal drug organization in the area?" Gibson abruptly changed the subject. "We have reason to believe that there is one here, working with the Mexican cartels."

"I don't know, I really know nothing about this," Gabriel said again. "If I did I would have told you already. You have to believe me, Asa."

Chapter 26

The interrogation of Gabriel and Grandpa Joe continued for another long hour, but they either really didn't know anything or they were very good liars. Asa wanted to believe that the man she had fallen in love with was innocent, but she was afraid that her feelings were going to make it difficult to objectively analyze the situation.

After the interview, Gibson took her aside, asking to talk to her.

"Listen to me, Asa," Gibson said gravely. "We should put our differences aside and work together to solve the case."

"Yes, I agree completely," she nodded. "We really should work hard to solve this mess. What do we have now? Anything new?"

"Actually, we might have something very important. The analysis of the soil samples matches the dirt we recovered from the Kimble Ranch," Gibson said, looking almost happy. "You know what that means, right? Combined with all the rest, we can say that Smith and Holliday were on the premises."

"But we already know that they were there. Uncle Joe told us that. What do you mean by 'all the rest' anyway?" Asa asked, "Did we get a match back on the shell casings?"

"According to the autopsy report, the two field agents were killed around the time they visited the Kimble Ranch. The old man didn't give us much, but we were able to determine that they were at the ranch about three weeks ago. At that same time, they were visiting all the farms and ranches in the area."

"That sounds logical," Asa agreed. "What else?"

"We matched the horseshoe print to several of the Kimble horses. I know that the same horseshoe make is found on many of the horses in the area, but it's still a solid lead."

"Yeah, you are right, but we still need a smoking gun." Asa shook her head. "What about the weapons? Did they match the bullets found in the agents?"

"So far, no." Gibson sounded really exasperated. "We retrieved three rifles, five pistols and who knows what else, but no ballistics match so far."

Todd and Asa decided to go back to the analysts and ask to retake the tests, hoping for something new to come up. Gibson had been right, the horseshoes were a perfect match to the print found near the abandoned car, but there were also many others. The horses in the Kimble's stable showed no other signs to having been near the killed agents, and that looked like another dead end.

The dirt samples were much better evidence, but they weren't able to find blood or any other evidence of the murders having been committed there. Gibson had searched everywhere, but everything must have been cleaned up really well after they had disposed of the bodies. They had found no evidence on their bodies either, no matter how carefully they looked. The killers had been either very lucky or very experienced.

"If it's an organized group, it shouldn't be a surprise that they know how to hide all traces of the crime," Asa said. "I have seen this happen before. In many cases, the organization will have people for everything, specializing. I was hoping we were dealing with an amateur organization here, with little experience in really serious crimes."

"I think they proved us wrong," Gibson agreed. "How could they operate under our noses and have no one notice anything?"

"Smith and Holliday did notice," Asa pointed sadly. "And they paid with their lives."

"Yeah."

"Yeah."

"What now?"

The question hung between them like a stone and neither of them knew how to answer it. They had some leads and had found a lot of small details about the case, but they still had nothing connecting the leads together; nothing to build the criminal case on.

"Agents," one of the analysts called them over. "I have been examining the parts of the bomb we found recovered from the building and noticed that all of the components could be purchased in a hardware store. I'm thinking the bomb brought such destruction because it was placed under the fuel tank in the basement."

"That is logical," Gibson answered. "Maybe we could trace the ingredients and find out who bought them."

"I'll make a list for you," the analyst said and the two agents walked away.

"Listen, Todd," Asa said. "I want to try and talk to Gabriel again. This time, I want some time alone with him. I think I might be able to convince him to talk to me."

"Asa, you can't let personal feelings guide you on this," Gibson said to her. "I've seen how you two look at each other. He might be totally innocent, but we still don't know that for sure and you have a job to do."

"You don't have to worry about that. I know what I'm doing. Actually, I intend to use what we have to make him talk."

"Make sure that this doesn't backfire, Asa." Gibson didn't look very convinced that it was a wise decision.

"I will, don't worry. You can trust me on this," Asa repeated.

She arranged for Gabriel to be taken into the back of the building, where they were away from other people. She watched him move as instructed but couldn't make herself go right away.

Asa's mind was filled with images of their time together and how sweet and gentle Gabriel had been. In those times, she couldn't have imagined that he might be bad. Now, even after everything that had happened, Asa felt the same. She still saw only the good in him and couldn't imagine him killing so many innocent people.

Chapter 27

Asa approached the small room where Gabriel was waiting and subconsciously adjusted her hair. The man was sitting with his back towards her and Asa had to circle him in order to face him. Gabriel watched her sit in front of him, but didn't speak. There was something tender in the way he watched her, and Asa felt the guilt that she was the one keeping him eat at her.

"Gabriel…" her voice trailed off.

"Asa, don't torture yourself, just do your job. I don't care. Seeing what those people are capable of, I understand why you acted the way you did. I had nothing to do with that bombing, but if you need to ask me more questions, just do it."

"I do believe that you had nothing to do with it, Gabriel, but you may know something that you don't even realize you know. There are documented cases of people who help solve crimes they believe they know nothing about," Asa tried to explain.

"That sounds great. What can I do for you?" The man adjusted his position on the chair and looked at her expectantly.

"Where were you when the two agents came to the ranch?" Asa opened her notebook and asked the first question.

"Me, David and Jane were all together away at the high pasture when that happened," Gabriel explained. "I cannot tell you the exact date, but we spent three entire weeks there. It was just before I met you in town. Actually, when I met you, we had just returned from the mountain."

"Okay, but can you swear that David and Jane were always with you? I mean, weren't there days or just hours, when they disappeared?"

"Entire days?" Gabriel repeated. "No, during the day we worked on separate pastures, but we usually met for dinner and always spent the night together in the same shelter."

"How long does it take to drive up there?" Asa asked the next question.

"Around two hours," Gabriel answered.

"Okay, two hours to get there, two hours to come back," she counted. "In other words, David would have enough time to drive back to the ranch and then back up the mountain without you noticing?"

"I… yeah… maybe, but I cannot believe that my brother is capable of doing something like that," Gabriel said somberly.

In another nearby room, Gibson was interrogating Grandpa Joe tirelessly. The old man was repeating that he knew nothing about the killings, but Gibson didn't give up. The agent continued the interview for another hour, but it was obvious that Grandpa Joe wasn't going to say anything different.

Both Kimble men had been interrogated tirelessly, pushed beyond their breaking point, and yet they got nothing. Asa felt defeated and Gibson wasn't looking any better. It was loser of a situation with no possible positive outcome.

"Gabriel, for one last time, do you know something about the bombing?" Asa tried one last time.

"I don't know anything," Gabriel repeated. "But, if you want I can get you to the high pasture camp to find the rest of my family. You will see then that we have nothing to do with all this."

"Okay, we'll start first thing in the morning," Asa confirmed and went out of the room to let Gibson know about the new plans.

"I'll get Grandpa Joe to the nearby hotel and leave an agent to watch him, you deal with Gabriel," Gibson said, as if that was the most natural thing in the world.

Asa watched him walk away and thought about what he had just said. *You deal with Gabriel… you deal with Gabriel.* Her mind continued to supply her with images from the previous several hours and all the ways she wasn't able to deal with Gabriel.

Following Agent Gibson's example, Asa Clark took Gabriel to the nearby hotel, which the FBI was using as headquarters at the moment. She put him into a secure room and went to make sure that the windows were locked and that he had no way to escape.

"I am not going to run, Asa," the man spoke from the door and the young woman watched him closely and locked the door behind her as she left. She pushed away the feelings that threatened to well up, and walked away making her mind go over the case. The way she felt about Gabriel Kimble could not be allowed to surface. She reminded herself that he could still he implicated in the killings and felt unbelievably sad.

Chapter 28

The next morning, Asa, Gabriel and a host of mounted police set off on horseback to the high pasture camp. The journey was long and everyone involved was well trained and prepared for it. Asa was the most inexperienced one, although the years spent on the reservation with her mother's family had prepared her for it.

Gabriel and Asa were at the head of the group, riding a few yards ahead of the others, so they could talk. The long journey was giving them plenty of time to discuss what had happened between them. Both of them had been silent and insecure that morning after a sleepless night.

Gabriel, on the other hand, was contemplating his own behavior and feeling angry for letting Asa make him act on feelings. He was still mad at her for hiding her identity and was angry at himself for not being able to see the truth for himself. Gabriel really liked her, but he loved his family, and apparently, Asa was here to destroy it.

"I think this is the time for us to talk about what happened," Asa was the first to speak. "I want to explain to you why I acted the way I did."

"I'm not interested in hearing more lies, Asa," Gabriel said. He spoke calmly, without even looking at her.

"I never lied to you, Gabriel," Asa said, shaking her head. "As I was saying, I was sent here to investigate the case of the two missing FBI agents, Agents Smith and Holliday. It was never in my plan to meet you or hide who I was. It simply happened."

"Well, it's never happened to me before, Asa, or to most of the people I know," Gabriel said, sarcastically.

"Nothing was as it was supposed to be. We had no leads and I was feeling powerless. Then my boss suggested that I get to know the locals a bit so I could get more information. The first time I went into a club I met you. You never asked who I was… I wanted to tell you more than once, but it never seemed like the right time."

"What about when you came to my home, when we spent the night together, when I took you on a date?" Gabriel asked. Asa could feel the hurt behind his words and wanted to tell him how she really felt, but it seemed too late now.

"During those moments, I wanted to be completely honest with you, but if you recall, we were doing other things. We weren't talking about much of anything. And anyway, I didn't want to mix my work with what we had. I was investigating a big case, Gabriel, and honestly, you were a distraction. That was until three days ago, when the soil we found in the car of the missing agents was found to be a match to the dirt around your ranch."

"Dirt? All this because of some dirt?" Gabriel was incredulous.

"Yeah." She nodded. "That was when we came to your ranch with the search warrant. Before that, I never suspected your family at all."

The woman turned around to look him in the eye, and waited for Gabriel to do the same.

"I'm sorry, Gabriel. I'm sorry for lying to you, for hurting you, for going after your family. I'm sorry about everything."

"Asa, though I understand what you are saying, I still can't help but feel hurt by your insinuations about my family," Gabriel pointed out. "I don't understand why it is so difficult for you to comprehend that we are just hard working cattle ranchers?"

"Because all the evidence points against it, Gabriel," she answered, exasperated. "I already told you that I only work with the evidence I have. I would never go after anyone if there was no good reason to do so."

"It's all circumstantial," Gabriel protested.

"No, no, all this evidence points against him," Asa commented. "You see, we have information that somewhere in this area there's a drug organization, and they're responsible for multiple acts of violence, and now for the bombing of the bank and the FBI field office."

"Asa, I would never do something like that, you've got to believe me," Gabriel pleaded.

"I know that, Gabriel," Asa answered. "I've always known that, and I want you to know that I will help you legally in any way I can."

"So that's your attempt to apologize again?" he asked again, sarcastically.

"No, this is my way of saying that I care about you, and that I believe you," Asa answered and let her horse fall behind. Gabriel turned around to look at her, but then concentrated on the road.

Gabriel was determined to show her that his family had nothing to do with the murders—or the bombing. It was true that his brother was intense sometimes, and his distrust of the system was well known, but Gabriel couldn't see his brother as a murderer despite all of that.

Asa watched his determined stance and thought that this man was really beautiful, especially when he was in his element, amidst the vast expanse of the Montana plains.

"Agent Clark," one of the policemen called to her.

"We'll be nearing the highlands soon. Do you want us to proceed from different directions?"

Asa thought about his proposition, but it seemed too soon to give such order, and she just shook her head.

"Let's get closer and see what the situation is. If the suspects refuse to talk to us, we'll think about other strategies. But for now, I want to give them the chance to provide an explanation."

Chapter 29

A few miles up, on the high pastures, David and Jane Kimble were having a beautiful moment together. It was one of those rare times when David was feeling romantic and was willing to forget all the grave problems of the world around them. He had used the morning to finish the work they had with the crop, and then had returned to the small cabin in the woods, where Jane was cooking lunch. He leaned against the wall of the cabin and watched her competently flip the steak, a simple thing perhaps, this wasn't a traditional kitchen.

"I'm sorry we have to work like this, Jane." He went on, "The ranch is gradually paying its way, but it's still going to be a long haul." She nodded and went on cooking. "I was just thinking back to when I inherited it, what a mess it was in. I don't know what I would have done if Martin Taylor, the neighbor wouldn't have giving me the idea of growing the other crops in order to save it. Yet, who knew things would get so difficult." Jane glanced at her husband.

"We do the best we can, David. You got drawn into the marijuana crop without realizing who you were dealing with." He moved over to where she was standing.

"With a bit of luck, this last crop will go and we'll be rid of them. I don't know what happened with Grandpa when we were away, but maybe it will all be finished. The crop will be gone and the agents will find nothing. We can become proper ranchers again and be happy. I hate all the secrecy." He moved closer. "We can be the couple we used to be, too."

"What are you doing?" the woman asked him innocently.

"I find it very cute when you play innocent, Jane, but we don't have time for that now." The man circled the table and walked closer to her, standing just inches away. Jane immediately recognized the look in his eyes and turned around, taking the food off the fire. David quickly pressed his chest against her back, successfully preventing her from doing anything else. They moved so that Jane was pressed against the wall of the cabin.

"David, please! I don't think we have time for that," Jane said in a shaky voice.

"I'm not doing anything you don't want me to do," the man replied, and ran his hands down her sides. Jane tried hard not to respond to either his words or his actions, but it was getting harder with each passing moment.

"David, I thought that we put an end to all this?" Her voice shaky and pleading.

"Jane, I'm sorry if I forced you to do something you didn't want to do," he said, sincerely, running his hand through his already messed up hair. It took Jane a few seconds to understand his words, as her mind was back to the time when she was the one playing with his hair.

"I know what you want, and I am sorry that I'm not able to give it to you," Jane said bitterly and opened one of the windows to look outside.

"Someone is coming up the mountain."

David felt almost physically hurt by the bitterness in her tone, but didn't comment on it. Jane was his other half and he hoped that she knew it.

Slowly, he exited the cabin and looked outside. A group of people was coming their way, but from that distance, David was unable to see who they were. One thing was for sure, few people knew this place, and even fewer came here uninvited. He went back into the cabin and took his rifle from behind the door.

Chapter 30

Jane followed David outside carrying a gun as well, determined to do whatever was needed to help her husband. She too, was aware that nothing good could come from the group of riders headed up the hill. She walked behind him. David had shown her a natural stone wall, situated to provide a perfect view of the path while providing protection to those hiding behind it. Their first thoughts were of poachers... come to take the crop from their fields.

David and Jane were able to finally recognize Gabriel riding in front, and Asa, right behind him. Behind them was a group of policemen on horseback, and David noticed that everyone—except Gabriel—was heavily armed.

"Why is Gabriel with all those FBI agents and police officers?" Jane finally gave voice to the question that was bothering both of them.

"Yeah, what is the FBI doing with my brother?" David asked. The mixed group of agents, officers and deputies were just over the hill at that time. David pointed the rifle at them and shouted, "What are you doing here?"

"David Kimble?" Asa shouted back, "David Kimble. We're here to talk to you. Come down, please?"

"Not before you tell me what is going on here," the man replied.

"Mr. Kimble, don't make things more difficult for yourself." Asa was all business again. "We need to ask you about the murders of two FBI agents, and the bombing of the bank building in Kalispell"

"I don't know anything about those things," David said angrily. "Get away from here."

"Listen, Mr. Kimble," Asa tried again. "You need to understand that—"

A gunshot took them by surprise. Asa and the police officers jumped down from their horses as they spooked and tried to find cover, but not all of them managed in time. Asa watched as two of the still-mounted officers fell to the ground, injured. She just hoped they weren't wounded too badly. The police team scrambled for secure positions and started firing back. A tense shootout erupted between the groups. Unsure of what to do next, Agent Clark searched for the only person there she really cared about. Gabriel was standing in his previous place and was desperately trying to calm the situation down.

"David! Stop shooting!" Asa heard him shout, and she hoped that his brother was going to listen to him.

A painful moan was heard from behind the stones and Gabriel started shouting louder. "David, are you okay? David, stop this madness!"

"Okay, okay, we are coming out." Everyone heard a woman's voice calling.

"Jane?" Gabriel called back. "Please, Jane, come out."

"Jane, this is Asa," Clark called too. "We just want to talk."

Gabriel started talking again, and finally was able to calm the tension and convince his brother and sister-in-law to give up their guns. The two of them came from behind the stones with their guns down and their hands in the air, surrendering. David was bleeding from his right arm, but his expression wasn't showing fear or pain. Jane was half hiding behind him, and Asa could see her eyes jumping from one person to the other in fear.

"David Kimble," Asa said. "You are under arrest under suspicion of the murders of two FBI agents, Agents Smith and Holliday; and for the bombing of the FBI field office in Kalispell; for resisting arrest and for shooting at FBI agents and police officers. You have the right to remain silent…"

Asa continued citing his Miranda rights as the other agents took their guns, searched them for more weapons and cuffed them securely. Neither of them resisted, and only Gabriel protested against the cuffs.

105

"My brother is injured," he said, pleading to Asa.

"He will be taken care of as soon as we make sure that there is no danger of more shooters," she assured him, and issued orders to close off the area and to take care of the injured. Fortunately, the two officers and David weren't badly injured, and the team was quickly able to provide emergency field care and immobilize their injuries until they could get down the mountain to a hospital.

Asa called in to the field office to both provide a status report on the operation, as well as request that an ambulance to wait for them at the foot of the mountain.

"Agent Clark," one of the mounted police officers reported to her. "The area is secure and there are no other threats."

Gabriel, who was close to her Asa, overheard the report and looked up, surprised by the news.

"What? No other people? What about Ezekiel? He was supposed to be with you as usual." His questions were addressed to David and Jane, but neither of them answered. Asa watched them as they remained tight-lipped and proud in their cuffs, and began to think they may not be as innocent as she wanted them to be, for Gabriel's sake.

She sighed almost painfully and felt relief that they had at least managed to take them into custody pending official charges.

"David," she turned towards the man. "What do you know about the murders of Agent Smith and Agent Holliday?" she asked.

"Nothing," he answered.

"Your grandfather told us that they came to your ranch around the time they were murdered," Asa insisted, and watched something like triumph shine in his eyes.

"I have nothing to say," the man insisted, and looked at his wife, who was silently crying beside him.

"Jane," Asa tried again. "Do you know something about this matter?"

"No, I know only what my husband knows," she said in a small voice.

"We want a lawyer."

"Oh, for God sake, tell them what they want to know. Tell them that you have nothing to do with all of this," Gabriel shouted at them. "Don't you see how serious the situation is right now?"

David Kimble just shrugged his shoulders at his brother's outburst, saying nothing, while Jane continued to cry. Asa had already realized that she wasn't going to be able to make them talk, so she focused her attention on taking them down to Kalispell. She left on the premise that three officers from the area who knew how to handle themselves in the mountain, would stay. They let Gabriel arrange for someone to come up and take care of the cattle until the situation was resolved, and only then began to head back.

About halfway down the hill, Asa got a radio call from Agent Todd Gibson, sounding very worried.

"Agent Clark," he yelled into the receiver. "We have an active shooter situation at the courthouse in Kalispell!"

"Do you know the identity of the shooter?" she asked, looking around. Everyone was listening to her conversation.

"Yes, according to the local police, the shooter is a neighbor and associate of David Kimble... Ezekiel Warren," Gibson explained.

"Okay, I know who he is," Asa confirmed, looking directly at David, who didn't even lower his eyes. "I'll be back in Kalispell in less than two hours, wait for me before you engage in anything too drastic."

Gibson agreed to do just that. For a while, the small group continued on their way in silence, but Gabriel couldn't take it anymore and spoke to his brother.

"Did you know that Ezekiel was shooting at people in Kalispell?"

David didn't answer, but that didn't stop Gabriel from asking again.

"Is that why you shot at us when you saw us coming? Please, David, tell me that you are not working with the cartel!"

Asa and the other officers watched the interaction in silence, feeling sorry for the younger man, who had just found out that his brother was a cold blooded killer.

As they reached the bottom of the mountain, Agent Clark received a call from the agents still investigating at the cabin. A large marijuana crop, probably valued in the millions, was found not far from the cabin—thousands of mature plants ready to harvest.

Chapter 31

Back in Kalispell, Ezekiel Warren had taken up a defensive position at the courthouse and was firing at the agents and at the police officers below. He had managed to injure one policeman and almost kill another, before everyone found cover. The shooting had been unexpected and in such a public place it had been hard to cut off the area and get the civilians to a safer place.

Agent Gibson was on the front line, working hard to find a way to stop the shooting without more casualties, but the man had chosen the perfect position and there was no way for the FBI or the police to reach him without putting themselves in danger. Therefore, a standoff had ensued until Agent Asa Clark could make it back into town and assume command.

Gibson thought that she must have been flying, because she arrived almost half an hour earlier than expected and immediately came to the place of shooting. Everybody made way for her, so the young agent was able to reach the front line in no time at all.

"Todd," she said to him, while crouching behind the car where he had taken up a position, "What's the situation?"

"Not good, if you ask me." The man shook his head. "The shooter has the highest position and is protected from all three sides. The only approach is from the front, and from there he's got a clear shot."

"When did this start?"

"About three hours ago," Gibson recounted. "According to the witnesses, he just showed up, climbed the tower and started firing on anyone in uniform. Two officers are injured, one pretty badly."

"God, when this is over we'll have the hospital filled with agents and police," Asa commented. "I see you have the snipers ready," she added, while scanning the positions of the three snipers strategically positioned on the roofs of nearby buildings.

"Yeah, we were waiting for you to start the communication

with him. I already tried to talk to him, but he just answered with more shots."

"Let's try that again," Asa decided. She took the megaphone from one of the agents standing nearby and looked up at the man, hiding in the tower.

"Mr. Warren," she called him. "My name is Asa Clark, we've met before. I need you to come down and surrender your weapon."

Everyone on the square fell silent as Asa waited for the man to answer. Two minutes passed, then five, but Ezekiel didn't answer and didn't move.

"Mr. Warren," Agent Clark started again. "We have your partners, David Kimble and Jane Kimble. Everything is over now, you should surrender. We found the plants."

A movement on her right side attracted Asa's attention, as she saw one of the FBI agents run from one car to another. At the same moment, three shots came from the tower, aimed at the agent.

"Shit," Gibson cursed beside her. "This is not going to work."

"Maybe I can help," Gibson and Clark turned around to see Gabriel Kimble standing behind them. "I should talk to him. He knows me. Let me try."

"Okay, but you should realize the danger you are facing?" Asa warned him.

"What can you tell us about him?"

"I don't know if I know anything useful or not, but I will tell you everything I know," Gabriel agreed. "He's an orphan, raised by the community. He has always lived here in rural Montana. His whole life is his ranch. Ezekiel Warren is a cattle rancher and a lifelong friend of my family. He was practically raised by our father and Grandpa Joe. He's a mysterious and quiet character, but that doesn't seem out of place to me at all. He is certainly not alone in that, living in this part of northwestern Montana. For all the years I've known him, Ezekiel has never shown interest in anything else.

"Yeah, sometimes we are blind when it comes to those closest to us," Gibson commented, and everyone around them agreed.

"Okay then, if you are sure you want to do this, let's try it," Asa said to him, secretly touching his hand as a way to show him she cared. "You'll stay behind the line of fire… and you'll wear a vest."

He agreed, and as he got outfitted, Asa issued orders to the snipers.

"Be ready, if you get an opening, take the shot."

Once Gabriel was dressed and prepared for the conversation, he stepped slightly from behind the car and spoke on the megaphone.

"Ezekiel, this is Gabriel. Gabriel Kimble," he spoke calmly. "Can I talk to you?"

"What do you want?" Ezekiel answered him.

"I wanted to ask you, why are you doing this? David and Jane are already arrested, and Grandpa Joe and I are being interrogated…so what is the point?"

"Don't you see? We were losing our ranches to the banks. We needed the money."

"Ezekiel, you killed people…"

"It was the Cartel. I was to keep the operation safe. Or they would deal with me."

Asa could see the man move on the tower and she whispered to Gabriel.

"Keep talking."

"Listen, Ezekiel," Gabriel continued. "You should—"

A loud shot was heard from behind them, and they all watched the man on the tower fall backwards.

"We got him," Gibson shouted, and ran towards the building. Every FBI agent and police officer was pointing a gun at the tower, while a number of special-forces agents climbed the stairs. Their plan to distract Ezekiel long enough for the snipers to get a clear shot had worked, and the shooter was dead.

Chapter 32

Ezekiel's body was carried away from the courthouse square under the watchful eyes of the nation… through the lenses of the local and national news agencies. The connection to the drug cartels had made the stories of the bombing and shootings all the more newsworthy, circling the entire nation in record time. Journalists from everywhere were coming to film the place and to interview the witnesses. Agent Asa Clark had already provided an official statement, naming Ezekiel Warren as the ring leader of the drug syndicate.

Grandpa Joe had finally broken down and admitted that he was part of the drug syndicate, trying to save the ranch. He had knowingly watched his son mismanage the ranch and had done nothing. After hours of interrogation, the old man had finally admitted that he had seen the two FBI agents killed and carried away, but he didn't show any remorse about it.

The interrogation of David and Jane Kimble was another difficult moment from that day. Asa and Gibson had seated them together in the same room, deciding that David would be more talkative if his wife was near him.

"Tell us about the murders of the FBI agents," Asa started, as soon as she was seated. "And don't try lying to us, because we already know the truth, we just need to compare a few facts."

"We aren't going to lie," David said stubbornly. "We aren't ashamed of our acts. We only did what had to be done."

"So, you admit that you killed the FBI agents?" Gibson joined the conversation. "Or should I phrase it differently. You were one of the many killers of the two agents."

"Yes, we were, we killed them. We didn't have a choice, the cartels ordered it. We couldn't say no to them. We waited for the agents to walk to the porch and start talking to Grandpa Joe. We already knew that they were coming to our ranch that day, they were working methodically, following a certain order, while visiting the ranches. So we were there, waiting for them."

"Should I ask, why did you kill them?"

"We were saving our livelihood. And if we hadn't done it, the cartel would have killed us," David added as an afterthought, looking directly at Asa.

"What about you, Jane, do you have the same reasons?" Asa gave the woman a way out, but Jane Kimble wasn't someone to run from responsibility. She had been looking at a point on the wall behind Asa and Gibson, not giving any sign that she was even listening to their conversation. Asa thought she had seen a tear fall at one point, but she couldn't be sure because of that stone-like expression.

"Jane, you have to answer me," Asa insisted.

"I don't have to do anything you say," the other woman almost spit at her. "You are the one responsible for all of this. You came into our lives and ruined them. Before the FBI came to our country, we were happy and carefree, but then you had to come and—"

"Okay, okay." Gibson interrupted her. "So you blame the FBI and Agent Clark for all the problems in your life. We got that. Now, tell us about the murders."

"We killed them all. I was there when we killed them. It was liberating." Jane sounded like someone who had been drugged.

"And the bombing?" Gibson continued.

"We did that too," Jane laughed, almost as a mad woman. "You are so stupid. You let us go right inside the building and put the bomb under the fuel tank without even searching us. And then, it was like a game."

"Jane, that is enough," David turned towards his wife and looked at her as if he didn't know her at all. Asa could understand how he was feeling. The woman acted as if she had lost her mind.

Hearing his voice, Jane trembled almost visibly, showing just how shaken the woman was. Asa saw the battle going on inside of her, and almost felt sorry for her. Jane didn't speak after that, but David gave them all the information they needed. Asa thought he realized it was all over and wanted just get on with it.

The next day, all the news reports were showing how David and Jane Kimble were hauled away in handcuffs, on their way to the federal prison. They were going to be tried as accomplices in the murder of the two FBI agents that were shot, the bombing of the bank building in Kalispell and resulting casualties, and likely for the murders of the three missing people, once thought to be unrelated incidents. At a minimum, they were going to be in prison for the rest of their lives. And, in a twist of irony, they would serve their time in federal protection, in order to protect them from the cartels. They had confessed to the murders of the two field agents, and to aiding in the bombing of the FBI field office.

Grandpa Joe was going to return home on house arrest, though he would also be tried for being part of the drug syndicate, withholding key evidence of the murders, and for lying to the FBI agents when interrogated.

The cameras were also there when Gabriel Kimble and Grandpa Joe were taken to a more secure location. Asa watched Gabriel hide his face, reminded that she had arrested his entire family. During the last twenty four hours, Agent Clark hadn't spoken Gabriel, but she could imagine how the man was feeling. Now that he had been taken away, she had to finish her reports on the conduct of the investigation, her least favorite part of life as an FBI agent.

Chapter 33

Gabriel was in local custody for a few days until the investigation was complete. Asa visited him a few times during that period, but her visits were kept short and professional. He had shown signs that he was ready to forgive her, but this time it was Asa who wasn't sure about her feelings.

When Gabriel Kimble was free to go home, Asa wasn't there to greet him, and she made sure to stay out of his way for a few days. It was one of the reasons she had traveled to the lake for a few days of relaxation.

She hadn't been around here for a long time, so Asa had a lot to see and explore. With a tourist book in hand, she explored some of the nearby sites, and two hours before sundown went to the lakeshore. She had heard wonderful things about the beauty of the lake here and wanted to enjoy it when there were fewer people on the beach.

That was when her phone suddenly vibrated, causing her to nearly drop it in surprise. She picked it up and read the message.

'How are you doing?' Gabriel had written.

'I'm good,' she typed back, feeling a bit self-conscious.

'What r u doing?'

Asa didn't answer for a few moments. She waited and waited, until Gabriel resent his message. *'What r u doing?'*

The simple letters on the screen made her feel excited again. The young woman had thought that she would be able to forget about him for at least a few hours, but here she was, once again entangled in his web. In the early days of their relationship, she had allowed herself to be hopeful, but then he had shown her what he thought of her and Asa had stopped dreaming.

Nodding to herself, Asa was about to put the phone away when another text made her eyes widen despite herself. She opened the phone and almost burst out laughing when she saw that he had sent a sad emoji. Getting the hint, she answered his question.

'I'm watching the lake.'

'U r by the lake????'

'Yeah!!!!' Asa answered with the same amount of punctuation if not emotion.

'Stop rolling your eyes, I can see you through the phone,' came the unexpected answer.

Asa decided that was enough messaging for the day and didn't answer him. Gabriel didn't give up though and continued to send message after message. Asa listened to the soft ping of her message tone, counting seven times. After ten more minutes, she couldn't resist the temptation anymore and opened the phone, going immediately to all the unread messages from Gabriel.

'What? U angry?'

'U r, aren't u?'

'I just know u that well.'

'U still there?'

'Stop ignoring me, Asa. :'('

'Hello!'

'Ok, see u...'

The last message was a bit of a surprise to her, but Asa just sighed, dropping her head back on the sand and looking up at the sky. She was about to give in and text him back, when someone sat down beside her. She turned her head to see Gabriel sitting beside her and looking at the lake.

"You worried me when you didn't answer my messages," the man said softly, as if afraid to disturb the peace on the beach.

"This was the first time you ever texted me," Asa answered in the same tone of voice. "What are you doing here?"

"I waited for you to answer..." his words sounded like an accusation.

"I needed some time for myself," Asa said and buried her feet deeper into the sand. They were almost alone on the beach, only three more people walking on the other side, but no one coming their way. She had wisely chosen one of the secluded sites on the lake line and had been enjoying the peace and quiet.

"Okay, but I thought you might be hungry," he said. Moving aside he revealed a paper bag full of little food containers.

"What did you bring?" Asa asked, sitting up to better see the food. Gabriel let her explore the contents of the bag and they ate the still warm Chinese food together, sharing the boxes and feeding each other.

Gabriel called it overly romantic, but kept offering her meat with his chopsticks. By the time their dinner was over, the sun had gone down and the beach was almost dark, illuminated only by the stars. Around that time, Gabriel had tugged her over to sit between his legs and was telling her a funny story about his college years.

"What did you do?" she asked him through her tears of laughter.

"Nothing, I simply waited for the morning, and when the maid came in, I asked her politely to untie me."

"It must have been the shock of her life," Asa commented.

"No, on the contrary, she told me that my predicament was nothing in comparison to what she had seen before." Gabriel shook his head. "And you should know that before untying me, she made sure to take a good look at my... you know."

Asa was enjoying herself. It seemed that seeing Gabriel was the only way she could relax these days. That thought surprised her and she looked at the man sitting behind her. He was watching her with amusement and Asa thought that he was trying to read her thoughts.

"Tell me something," she gathered the courage to ask. "Why do you keep coming back if you despise me so much?"

"I never said that I despise you," Gabriel stated, suddenly very serious. "I may not trust you, and I may be angry with you for using me, but Asa, I never hated you. On the contrary, I really like you... a lot."

"I've told you over and over that I didn't want to deceive you, and that I let it go too far, but I also had a job to do. Lives were at stake… even more than I knew." the woman insisted.

"Well, you might not be completely trustworthy, but you sure are different from all the other women in my life. I still find it hard to forget what we shared."

"You're being honest with me, aren't you?" Asa changed her position and faced him. "Do you really believe me now?"

"Yes… you put it quite right," Gabriel nodded.

"I don't like it," Asa shook her head instead. "I hate the idea of being away from you."

"So, you don't want to take a break?" he asked.

"Break from what?" Asa asked him. "It seems like there is always going to be something special between us no matter what we choose to do or not do, so, there is really nothing to take a break from."

"If you say so," Gabriel agreed.

"In that case, what do you want to do next?" he asked out of nowhere, surprising both of them with the change of subject.

"I think I need a drink now," Asa answered. "Let's go to a bar."

Gabriel nodded his head in affirmation and helped her to stand. Together they gathered the take out containers and trash, then headed toward his car. Asa was walking beside him, and realized that the terrible feeling of doom she'd carried in her heart for so long wasn't there.

On their way back to Kalispell, Asa decided that she should update Gabriel about what was going on with his family.

"So, all the indictments against your brother and Jane have been filed now, as far as I know. Looks like Grandpa Joe will probably be released, even though he's still vowing to take revenge on the government for hurting his family."

"Don't worry," Gabriel quickly added. "Grandpa Joe isn't a threat to anybody. He's pretty much all talk and no action at this point."

"I know, don't worry, I was the one who vouched for him," Asa assured him.

"What will happen to the ranch?" Gabriel asked.

"I don't know. The marijuana was on federal land, not the ranch. But the assets of those involved in the drug trade are often seized. Plus, it looks like your father and then your brother owed the banks a lot of money. They may try to foreclose on the property even if the feds don't seize it."

"I never knew about the money situation—never asked and was never told. I guess I should have paid more attention to the ranch."

Chapter 34

There was a light dusting of dirt on the pavement. Looking at the remains of the bank building while feeling the sharp chill in the air caused Gibson pull his jacket tighter around himself. Painful memories gripped Todd as he walked down the deserted street. Replaying the last few weeks; Smith and Holliday disappearing, the arrival of Agent Asa Clark, the bombing of the bank building, which took out the FBI offices and several dozen casualties, including the Deputy Director.

Gibson wasn't tired. He wasn't. He was just fed up and ready to give up. Nothing in life made sense anymore and he wanted just to hide somewhere and rest.

Nothing had changed since Deputy Director Josie Shepherd had called him over two months ago. They had been friends and it still wasn't feeling right. Gibson should be happy now. He had a good job, which he loved and he was healthy, and that was all that mattered. And yet, he wouldn't let himself be happy, he wouldn't let himself ruin things again by infecting others with his own conflicted feelings.

But no matter how hard he tried, he couldn't rid himself of these thoughts. Shepherd's face swam at the forefront of his mind, smiling gently at him. These feelings had nested in his brain like some sort of disease, filling him with agonizing loneliness.

Gibson continued up the street until he reached the new FBI field office, now set in another building. There was no one in sight except for the clerk behind the front desk. As he walked down the empty hall towards his office, fluorescent lights made him squint as he passed Asa Clark's office on the way. Thinking better of it, he turned and went back.

"Rough night?" he asked her as he scanned the office and noticed the shadows under her eyes.

"Yeah, you could say that," Asa said, emotionlessly, taking

the file the man handed to her.

"Take care of yourself, Asa." Gibson sat down on the chair that she'd pointed to, feeling exhausted. "I wanted to congratulate you on a job well done."

Asa smiled sadly at the praise. "Thank you, we really did an excellent job, but it's hard to feel good about it when we lost so many. I am so disappointed that we lost Josie Shepherd and all the other agents. All I want is for them to be alive and back here with us."

"I know, I feel the same way," the man agreed with her. "But, there's nothing we can do for them now, except do our jobs well in their memory."

It was only a week ago that they had attended the funerals of the FBI officers who perished in the bombing at the Kalispell field office. During the ceremony, Agent Clark had spoken about the dedication of the people who had met their death in the horrible flames of that fire.

"What are your plans for the future, Todd?" Asa asked, as she offered him a glass of scotch. "I'm thinking I'll stay here in Kalispell a little longer."

"Really? I wasn't expecting you to want to stay here..." Gibson wondered.

"Me neither, but you know how it is. I want to reconnect with my Salish roots and, well... I want to see if my relationship with Gabriel has any future," Asa confessed, feeling the color rise on her face.

"Gabriel Kimble" the man repeated. "I'd like to be here to see how you'll go about making an honest man out of him, but unfortunately, I've been asked to move to Salt Lake City."

"Oh, Salt Lake, huh. Does that fit in with your plans for the future?" Asa asked, feeling a bit sorry that Todd would no longer be working with her. Their relationship had changed completely during the last few weeks and they had reached a point where they could genuinely call each other friends.

"Yes, I am relocating to the FBI office in Salt Lake City for a promotion," Gibson explained proudly. "I didn't ask for it, but since they're offering, I'm not going to say no. I can't say that I'm against the idea of a change just now. You know, new scenery, new cases, and plenty to keep me busy. Did I tell you about the time I was sent here? They told me it will be just a temporary assignment, and that I'd be transferred in no time. Go figure, after God knows how many years, I'm still here, waiting for that transfer."

Asa laughed at the way he looked at his life and thought that only a few weeks ago it would have been impossible. Agent Todd Gibson had finally accepted her as a friend. A few days ago, he had suggested that Gabriel Kimble might be the right man for her, if she could manage to keep him in line. He had even expressed his concern about how she was going to manage a rancher like him and her FBI job.

Asa still didn't know all the answers, but one thing was sure, she had all the time in the world to figure it out. Gabriel had forgiven her, and was going to work at trying to keep the ranch in the family. Gibson had accepted her… as a fellow agent worthy of the title, and now… it was her turn to decide what she wanted.

"A toast." Agent Gibson raised his glass. "Let's drink for those who lost their lives in this horrible affair. Let's drink for Deputy Director Shepherd and for Ann, and for all the others. Let's drink for our future and for what life is going to throw our way. We could easily have lost our lives that day, but since we didn't… we need to live well in honor of those who did."

"Well said," Asa said, as she joined him.

Gibson stayed to chat for few minutes more, and then went to his office to put things in order. He was given another week to help the new Agent in charge of the office settle in, and then was he supposed to take two months' vacation. He really didn't know what to do with it, but his superiors had insisted and now he was even looking forward to it in a way.

He entered the office, but it didn't feel like home. It was too new, too impersonal for his taste. The old office had been filled with memories, photos, mementoes and small pieces of history, something that Gibson really missed.

Chapter 35

Gibson had left Kalispell two weeks earlier and agent Asa Clark was slowly adjusting to her new way of life. Gabriel had asked her to move in with him at the ranch and eventually Asa had agreed, although it felt strange.

"Look, it doesn't seem right for me to live here," she had tried to tell him. "This is David and Jane's home, and I'm the one responsible for putting them in prison."

"Don't worry. We'll redecorate and make some changes so it will be ours. I may end up losing it anyway, but either way, it will never be theirs again, no matter what you or I do, so it isn't like we're taking their home. I love my brother... and Jane," he had added quickly. "But, I love them as they were before all of this money drug business took over their lives. Their minds are twisted with greed and hatred. I want nothing to do with the people they have become. They made their own choices... terrible choices."

"You can't just cancel them from your life though," Asa had protested. "They are still your family."

"I'm not going to do that, don't worry. I intend to visit them in prison, but only when they come to understand just what they've done, and begin to show some remorse." Gabriel had smiled sadly then.

"What about Grandpa Joe? He won't be happy to see me at the ranch." Asa had found another reason to decline his offer.

"I've spoken to his doctor." Gabriel looked sad again. "My grandfather is suffering from Alzheimer's, and apparently a form where the dementia progresses very quickly. They can't predict these things for sure, of course, but according to this doctor him, in less than a year, it is likely that he won't recognize me anymore, and will ultimately lose all of his memory."

"This is rather sudden, isn't it?"

"Yes, the stress of the past months, coupled with the trauma of the murders he witnessed, and the horror of the bombing. Then Ezekiel killed, David and Jane destined for prison, it's all been too much for his brain which was already battling the disease.

"I am so sorry. He seems to be such a sweet character underneath all the bluster." Asa had given him a hug. "What are you going to do now?"

"There is a farm, just outside Kalispell, which someone converted into a retirement home for people just like Grandpa Joe. I think that he'll be happy there, especially since there are a few of his old friends there. His older memories are intact for now so he'll be able to swap stories with them and such. These facilities are used to their patients having some radical tendencies, so it should work out."

"And what else?" Asa couldn't help asking.

"Someday, after things settle down a bit, I'd like to take a trip, and see some of the world beyond Montana. I was thinking we would find someone to take care of the ranch, assuming I still have it, and we will go away for a few months," Gabriel offered. "Would you come with me?"

"Hell yes." Asa jumped at his offer and threw herself at him.

Just now, they were attending the celebration of life at the nearby Flathead Indian Reservation. Every year, the American Indians of the area held a beautiful ceremony near Flathead Lake, where they thanked nature for everything provided to them throughout the year.

Asa had been invited and she extended the invitation to Gabriel, wanting to share this beautiful moment of gratitude with him. They both had a lot to be thankful for and Gabriel had happily attended.

They had officially resumed their relationship and now had the ranch to look after together. Asa had taken a permanent position at the Kalispell office, all the while thinking that the late Deputy Director Shepherd would not be happy with that. But Asa had other priorities and Gabriel was now the most important thing in her life.

It was fitting that the nature they celebrated was beautiful that day.

Asa and Gabriel were completely and utterly in love, although the words had never passed their lips. Asa was afraid to open herself completely to him, and Gabriel wasn't sure if she was on the same page. Asa wondered if he would ever love her and Gabriel was afraid to admit that he did.

An old Indian woman approached them. "You look happy together," she said, her heavily lined face a thing of beauty when she smiled. "Just don't forget that such happiness is founded on mutual respect and honesty."

Chapter 36

Two months later…

Asa walked up the stairs, leaving Gabriel to finish his work in the barn. The young woman found her way to the second floor and looked out the windows for a while, admiring the beautiful garden and the starry sky. Her new home was everything she could hope for and Asa was happy to live in it, and yet…

She was still feeling as if Gabriel was holding something back, and even after those weeks they spent together, he still wasn't able to forgive her.

Suddenly two hands held her against the window's edge, basically trapping her, while leaning forward to speak in her ear.

"Is it already midnight?" Asa recognized Gabriel's voice, before she had the chance to turn around and protest. "I thought only Cinderella had to leave the ball so early?"

"My place may not be here, Cinderella or no Cinderella," Asa said sadly, refusing to take the bait.

"I couldn't take my eyes off of you all day," he whispered, dipping his tongue into her ear. "You must know we are meant for each other."

"I thought you couldn't stand me?" Asa answered, for a brief moment wondering if she was imagining his words.

Gabriel didn't answer her, but raised his hand to absently rub her belly, as it tingled under his hand.

"You think you can fool me, don't you?" he whispered, his lips touching her neck. "If you really want to know what I think, I will tell you. You managed to entangle me and now I am unable to keep my hands off you."

Asa pulled back jokingly, "I think I want to go now." Gabriel nodded and let her head towards the stairs, following her silently.

"We need to talk, Asa."

"Right now?" She turned around to look at him.

"Yes, right now," the man repeated and, without further discussion, tugged her towards the nearest room, which turned out to be a small parlor, rarely used. Asa froze, when she realized that Gabriel was very serious. Maybe there was something bad that he hadn't confessed.

The outside world was a dull white, and with both the hunger to touch and be united, as well as the desire to kill each other, Asa and Gabriel didn't care for anything else. Asa shook her head slightly and turned to look at him.

"I don't even know what we are doing here," she said seriously.

Gabriel's eyes were focused on her lips and Asa saw them grow hungrier. Asa's own eyes widened as she watched him get closer. It was happening again. She was once more going to fall victim to his charm and let him take whatever he wanted. He knew it and she knew it too. It was like a bad movie, one she didn't like, but couldn't stop watching, nevertheless. Was sex the only thing that kept them together?

It was Gabriel who closed the small distance between them and pressed his lips against hers, his mouth hot and insistent. Asa made a noise of surprise, which was quickly muffled as his tongue pressed into her mouth. She tried to pull away, panting.

Right there, just like that, that was what she wanted…

"What are you doing?" She sputtered, though her voice wasn't angry or indignant. Instead, it was full of the old wonder. She touched her lips, feeling the wetness left from Gabriel's kiss.

"Sit down," Gabriel gasped. "I'm sorry for acting like an asshole."

Asa sat on the only sofa in the room, while Gabriel started pacing silently.

"What is it, now?" Asa couldn't wait any longer. She waited for him to look at her and made a move to get up. She was finding it hard to think when he was so close, so she needed to put some distance between the two of them.

Gabriel frowned. "Stay," he said urgently. Asa sighed and the man licked his lips as he watched her carefully. "I wanted to say that your appearance in my life surprised me and I acted... I acted... You know how I acted..."

Asa gave him a hard look. "You accused me of going after you, and then you treated me like trash..."

"Yes." The man shook his head and walked over to her. He stood there, just looking down at her, his eyes meeting hers. "I know I was wrong."

"Really?" the woman asked sarcastically. "And what made you change your mind?"

Gabriel licked his lips, the tip of his tongue resting for a moment on his lower lip. "I think I always knew it, but it was easier to accuse you than to admit that fate was playing with us."

"Fate?"

"What do you call it, if not fate? We met without knowing who we were..."

"Okay, okay," Asa interrupted him. "What now?" She didn't particularly like the idea of him thinking that it was fate that put them together. She preferred to see it all as a good experience that grew out of a bad one.

"Is something wrong?" Asa asked again.

"Everything is wrong," Gabriel said sadly.

"The ranch..." he started.

"I like your ranch..."

"And I love you..." Gabriel said, matching her tone of voice, "but we have lost the ranch."

Finally hearing what she had been longing for, Asa looked him in the eye.

"I love you too, with or without a ranch, Gabriel."

The smile that illuminated his face was the only answer she needed. Finally, what she had been missing was found, and without reservation, she ran into his arms.

The End

Sample Story

<u>Killed</u> by James Kipling

http://www.amazon.com/gp/product/B00H39Y6ZQ

It was around three in the morning when I got the call. I didn't want to answer. Despite the internal struggle to fight the urge to wake up, I groaned and sat up. I picked up the cell to confirm what I had feared most ... work was calling. I clicked the green button on my phone and opened the line. "Walker, here."

"I need you out here, right now," the voice on the other end pretty much commanded. I could tell from the lack of small talk that it was my boss. I doubt he enjoyed being up this early either. Part of me wanted to tell Captain George Bancroft where to go, and it wasn't Kokomo. But I resisted for one simple reason, and it was how he'd structured the command: "I need you."

Captain Bancroft didn't ask for help often. Usually, he was diplomatic if he was asking us to do extra work to help when they were burdened with too many cases at one time. It was this personal request that gave me the impression that whatever was going on was very serious.

"Where are you?" I asked as I picked up my watch to confirm how early it was.

There was a short pause. "I'm at the station. That's not where the job is."

"And where is that?" I quickly asked.

"State University, East Campus," he answered.

The captain knew exactly what kind of response I would give, as within seconds I was more awake than I'd ever thought was possible at that time of the morning on an off day. "I'm on my way."

"They're at the Arts building," Captain Bancroft continued.

"You should be able to navigate your way from there. Just follow the lights. I'll get down there as soon as I can. I've been told it's a pretty brutal murder."

"All right," I answered. "I'll get out there as soon as I can."

"Thank you."

After the line went dead, I immediately called my brother and hoped he wasn't out drinking. Thankfully, he was also asleep. "Jake?" he barely spat out.

"Clive, get your ass over here," I quickly shot back. "I've been called into work and it's pretty serious."

"How fucking serious could it be?" he asked, grumpy and clearly unhappy he was being disturbed so early.

"I've been called to Cassie's campus," I quickly answered. "Get your ass over here, now!"

There was a short pause. "I'll be there in five minutes."

Clive was actually over at my place in less than three minutes, and I appreciated his hustle. I hadn't heard from Cassie in over a week, so to be called to her campus was making my heart race a little. Clive could tell and didn't fuck around, scooting over to my place as quickly as he could. He always crashed on the couch and made pancakes for the girls whenever I was called to work. They loved their uncle and knew he only subbed in when things were tense and required my help. It rarely happened, but I wasn't going to turn my back on them this time, not when the location of the crime scene was so personal.

As I drove, the worst case scenario kept flashing through my head: Cassie was dead and I was being called in to identify the body. It was always my worst nightmare, to be the officer on the scene only to find out it was my own girl underneath the black canvas.

For some reason, my subconscious loved to torment me with

the worst possible scenario, ever since the girls had been babies. I'd often had nightmares about leaving the babies on the bus and running after it as it drove away with my kids inside; then, I'd wake up in a pool of sweat. As the girls got older, my dreams became scarier. From getting into a car accident whenever one of them was learning to drive, to coming upon a crime scene and finding that my own child is the victim.

My brain just wasn't willing to cut me some slack. I'd been a dad for over 21 years and the girls were alive and well. All fingers and toes were still attached and none of them even sporting a tattoo; so deep down, I had to admit that I must have done something right.

That never stopped the dreams, though, and I was reminded of them as I drove to the East Campus, hoping that I was not driving towards my worst fear. As I pulled into the main parking lot in front of the Arts building, I could see what the Captain was talking about. There were several cop cars there, lights flashing and people being kept at bay. Reporters, students, and various onlookers wanted to know what was going on. As I pulled in, I could see Flo in the distance talking to a few medics. They were most likely forensics or from the coroner's office, ready to pick up a fresh body.

But I got an even bigger surprise, as much to my relief, I saw Cassie waving. She recognized my car and must have had a feeling I'd be here. It was likely that she, and many other students, had all walked over from the dormitories to see what the hell was going on. Once I got out of the car, I walked over to where Cassie was and gave her a big hug. I had feared the worst and it was so good to see her. "What are you doing out here?"

"I'm with my friends, I'll be fine," Cassie answered. "I also thought you might be out here, too. I didn't want you to panic."

Cassie was one smart girl. She knew I would have been panicking on the inside, especially if no one had told me what was really going on. I put a hand through her long hair and smiled. "Stay back and don't get too close. I want you guys to head back to the dorm in 10 minutes. Understood?"

"Yes, sir," she replied with a hint of sarcasm. I could tell she had no intention of listening to a single word I said. She was 21 and living on her own. She called the shots and I was just a part time parent she saw when she needed a little extra cash and an urge to crash or do laundry at my place.

Relieved that my worst dreams had not become a reality, I was able to take a deep breath and finally get back to work. I quickly walked over to where Flo was, and she could tell from how I was interacting with Cassie that I hadn't been told very much. "You should have called me," she quickly started. "I would have confirmed it wasn't Cassie. It's not even a woman."

"It's not?" I called back to her. That was odd. Most of the time when we responded to a homicide, it was a woman. Usually when men got into a tussle, they just bruised each other up and then went their separate ways. Rarely did it ever come to us.

I followed Flo to the side of the Arts building where there was a narrow path between that building and the science hall. That's where the tarp was, and I could tell by the officers there that this wasn't going to be a pretty sight. The Captain never kept people back unless it was something he didn't want on the front page. The kind of sight the police would prefer to keep out of the limelight since this was someone's son, someone's brother.

I walked up to the tarp, knelt down beside it, and quickly lifted the canvas to take a peek. It was way more gruesome than I'd imagined. The victim was on his stomach, bound and gagged with one of those rubber balls that had straps. It was a common item ... something that you can get at any sex shop. There would be no point trying to trace it. The victim's hands were bound behind his back with a pretty solid pair of handcuffs. I looked at his back and then back up at Flo. "Someone hit him with a Taser."

"I noticed that, too," Flo confirmed. "It would explain how he managed to get the victim bound without a fight."

"How many stab wounds are there?" I quickly asked as I noticed the obvious cause of death. After being bound by his assailant, it was clear enough that the boy had been knifed to death, as there were several lacerations in his back.

"I counted over twenty stab wounds," Flo answered.

"Not a nice way to go," I replied as I kept looking. There was blood coming out of every wound. "This wasn't a quick killing. Whoever did this made sure it was slow and very painful. He was tortured."

I lifted the tarp to see the real reason why the victim had been covered in the first place. His pants and underwear had been pulled down to his ankles. "Damn," I said as I put the tarp back down. "The blood from his anal cavity suggests that he was sexually assaulted. The flow also suggests that the assault occurred prior to his stabbing. It would explain the need for a ball-gag."

"So he could rape the victim without having to keep a hand over his mouth," Flo said as she connected the dots. I could tell why Captain Bancroft had wanted me out here: this homicide was going to generate a lot of media based on how brutal it was.

"It would appear so," I concurred. "This boy suffered a great deal before he died. It would suggest that it might have been personal."

"Maybe it's just a psychopath?" one of the officers suggested.

"I sure hope not," Flo quickly countered. "If it's personal, then this is likely a one-time thing. Psychos leave a much higher body count."

"Any cameras?" I quickly asked.

"Not in this corner," Flo answered. "It's a massive blind spot back here."

"I was afraid of that," I called back as I stood up and started to walk around. Committing a crime this brutal in the one spot where not a single camera could see it wasn't the kind of thing I wanted to see. This person was not only quick and brutal, but also smart. "Either the killer took the time to scout this area out long before the crime was committed, or he's a student and lives here."

"I don't like those options," Flo frankly confessed.

Before I could say something else, the Captain came over to speak with us. I could tell that, like me, he wasn't very impressed with the scene. His anger was a little more projected than my disgust so I could tell he knew something that I didn't. "What do you know?" I quickly asked.

"The victim's name is Wally Bennett." The Captain handed over a small bag that contained evidence. "We found his wallet just around the corner. The killer dumped it in the trash can. I'm going to have forensics dust it for prints."

"You're not going to find any," I quickly called back. "This killer is too meticulous to leave something like a print lying around."

"We'll check anyway, just to be sure," Captain Bancroft replied defiantly.

"Bennett," I said to myself. "Why does that name that sound familiar?"

"You don't watch much sports, do ya, Jake," the Captain replied.

"With three girls, not really," I confessed. "I take it this Wally isn't just your ordinary student, then?"

"Try the star quarterback," the Captain answered. "The media is going to freak out when they find out who's here."

"You have no idea," Flo chipped in. I was thinking the same

thing but had restrained myself from voicing that opinion out loud.

"What is she talking about?" the Captain asked.

"You haven't taken a look?" I asked, gesturing to the canvas.

"I haven't," the Captain replied. "How brutal was it?"

"Very," Flo answered.

"On a scale of 1 to 10?" he asked.

"Spinal Tap," I answered. It was not the answer he wanted to hear but it was my way of telling him that out of 10, this was an 11 on the gross-out meter.

"Shit," he muttered as he took out a cigar and lit up. I grabbed his arm and pulled him away from the scene a bit to speak. "What the fuck happened?"

"Based on what I've seen, the victim was tazed and then dragged to this spot because it's a blind spot to all the cameras," I started.

"Fuck, then the killer knows this place," the captain replied.

"It would suggest that," I agreed, "but it could also suggest that the killer did some advanced scouting, which would suggest extreme premeditation. We can't rule out either at this point."

"How was he killed?"

"He was bound and gagged and then stabbed over twenty times." I paused for a moment. "It looks like he was also sexually assaulted."

"Jesus Christ," Captain Bancroft said. He looked like he was going to vomit. "So what you're telling me is that our star quarterback was bound, gagged, raped, and then stabbed to death?"

"That about sums it up."

"Fuck me."

"We'll know more when we get the autopsy report."

"This kid was guaranteed a spot in the NFL-"

"It looks personal," I interrupted, refusing to let that detail distract me. "Whoever did this wanted Bennett to suffer. The whole point of using the gag was to make sure he couldn't make a sound when being raped. The killer wanted him awake, to feel everything."

"Son of a bitch," the Captain cussed again. This was the last thing he needed on his plate. He had gotten word that it was brutal, but he wasn't prepared for it to be this bad.

"We need to start talking to his friends," I suggested.

"Need to see if anyone was following him," Flo added. "Or if anyone was sending threats to him by mail or email."

"We'll start rounding people up," the Captain said, unable to take his eyes off the tarp. Underneath it was the worst media image he could ever imagine. Tabloids and news outlets were going to have a field day with this one. "How much of this can we keep under wraps?"

"I'm not sure," I honestly replied. "There's only so much we can hold back. The last thing we want to do is downplay it only to have another body turn up."

"That's not what I wanted to hear," the Captain replied.

"We have to prepare just in case." I could tell just the thought of a serial killer was making the Captain very, very nervous. Before, when we'd had to deal with a serial killer in our city, the last guy in charge of homicide lost his job. Captain Bancroft was his replacement. Now it was his turn to be in the hot seat and he didn't relish the thought of having to fight for his job. High profile cases tended to put the spotlight on the entire department, so he wasn't the only one nervous about this.

"All right." The Captain took one more deep puff and then

put out his cigar before putting it back into his coat pocket. "I'll take care of the media. You and Flo find this piece of shit and do it quickly."

"What do we do now?" Flo asked as she walked over.

"We should let forensics do their thing and get the body the hell out of here as soon as possible." I made a motion to one of the buildings. "We need to speak with the Dean as soon as possible, also." As we left the crime scene for forensics to go over, I could see the flashes and questions being yelled at our Captain as he fielded questions from the media.

I could hear him making the usual statements: all measures were being used to find whoever did this and our best people were on the case. Thanks, Chief, no pressure. We crossed over to the administration building that was a short skip from the Arts building where the body had been found. It was around six in the morning, but a lot of people were in, thanks to the events going on outside. I slowly walked up to the main desk and flashed my badge. "Detective Walker to see the Dean."

"Yes, sir," the secretary said as she picked up a phone and made a call. A few seconds later, she put it down. "Both the Dean and the President of the University are waiting for you in his office."

"Thank you," I said as I walked away and down the hall. I had been here a few years ago when I'd registered Cassie. I also knew my way around because I'd graduated from this place before joining the force. I knocked on the door and was called to enter. "Gentlemen, I'm Detective Jake Walker, and this is Detective Florence Harris."

"Pleased to meet you," the Dean said as he stood up from his desk and shook our hands. "I'm Richard Jackson, Dean of Arts. This is Oswald Butler, the University's President. We are deeply saddened by what is going on here."

"Have you identified the body?" President Butler asked. It was clear he was concerned the victim might be a student, and was most likely hoping it was a homeless man that had just happened to be in the wrong place at the wrong time. Still bad for the image, but nothing compared to a student getting killed.

"We have," I answered. "He's a member of your student body."

"Who is it?" Dean Jackson then asked.

"We need to speak with the football coach," I stated.

"Shit," President Butler said. A high profile student didn't make this easier.

"He's a member of the team," I filled in. "It's the quarterback. We need to know if anyone has been making any threats against any players on the team. I realize college sports can be competitive, but any threat sent in could be a clue that will lead us to a suspect."

"What are you trying to find?" the Dean then asked.

"We need to make sure that no other players are at risk," Flo replied. "We have to make sure that there isn't someone out there who is gunning for the whole team, or to establish if he had a personal vendetta with the victim."

"I'll talk to the coach and our IT people. If anything was flagged by them, I'll have them sent to your station," President Butler answered. "We don't want anyone else to get hurt, so we'll get this taken care of as soon as possible."

"I appreciate that," I said as I fished a card out of my wallet and placed it on the Dean's desk. "Call me if you guys find anything. We'll be in touch."

As we left the office, I had a feeling this was going to be more political than anything else. I'd been playing dumb with the Captain back at the scene when talking about football. My brother was a die-hard college football fan and I remembered a lot of things he'd told me about this upcoming season.

Wally was a candidate for the college player of the year. If he even lived up to half the hype going into this season, he was going to be a top 10 pick at next year's draft. A promising career had been brutally cut short by someone who didn't like him very much. The murder was too vicious to be someone from a rival team. Whoever committed this heinous act clearly hated Wally a great deal, to the point where he'd tortured the poor boy for at least a half hour before finally putting him out of his misery. "We need to speak with the victim's family. See if they were getting any threats, as well."

"Think this one is personal, Jake?" Flo called back from a few stairs behind.

"It sure looks like it," I answered, but as I said that to her, I noticed something out of place. One of our people from forensics was in the lobby. They were looking for me, and I knew exactly what that meant: they'd already found something.

http://www.amazon.com/gp/product/B00H39Y6ZQ

Thank You

Dear Reader,

Thank you for choosing to read my books out of the thousands that merit reading. I recognize that reading takes time and quietness, so I am grateful that you have designed your lives to allow for this enriching endeavor, whatever the book's title and subject.

Now more than ever before, Amazon reviews and Social Media play vital role in helping individuals make their reading choices. If any of my books have moved you, inspired you, or educated you, please share your reactions with others by posting an Amazon review as well as via email, Facebook, Twitter, Goodreads, -- or even old-fashioned face-to-face conversation!

I invite you to connect with me on Facebook:
https://www.facebook.com/AuthorJamesKipling/

With profound gratitude, and with hope for your continued reading pleasure,

James Kipling
Author & Publisher

g

Made in the USA
Monee, IL
07 January 2021